Nothing for you my dear

Still i love you....!

Nothing for you my dear

Still i love you.....

Arpit Dugar

Srishti
PUBLISHERS & DISTRIBUTORS

Srishti Publishers & Distributors
Registered Office: N-16, C.R. Park
New Delhi – 110 019
Corporate Office: 212A, Peacock Lane
Shahpur Jat, New Delhi – 110 049
editorial@srishtipublishers.com

First published by Srishti Publishers & Distributors in 2009
13th impression
Copyright © Arpit Dugar, 2009

ISBN 9788188575749

Typeset in AGaramond 11pt. by Suresh Kumar Sharma at Srishti

*To my very loving parents
my friends
and the girl who stood by me all the times.*

Acknowledgment

Hey just dangle on for 100 seconds here, in case you are pondering that this is just my book. In my case, all the characters which you will face had been true supporters of mine, it's a synergistic product of many minds. In particular I would like to thank:

Mummy and Papa – for their inestimable uphold. Bhayia – he is the man of my life, an ideal bro...friend and everything! My beautiful Bhabhi and wonderful sis can't be left out as they served me snacks and chinos at all the odd times......eh!

My best friends Nishant (*Heil Hitler*), Dushyant *(Bhushand)*,Astha (*Ghaskha*), Prashant Bhayia (*The Dude*) and Rashmi (*Chotu)* and friends – Smriti, Manoneet, Nitin, DC, Zoya, Abhishek, Trishna and Chacha. Without you, this book would be nowhere.....*after all you all have to buy its copies and also promote it.* Thank you for helping me snoop around fortuitous places, gathering ideas, providing information, stealing various catch lines and arranging so much of stuff. Most importantly, thank you for sharing your experiences with me, trusting blindly on me and inspiring me at all stages of life.

My life when I worked frenziedly for my college was living strain, but probably the *jhakkas* phase of my life. But the Discipline Committee forced me to wonder why this was happening to me. Now I know. Without that experience I could not have done this book. I owe my sincere thanks to the management of the college and all the faculties whom I have been in touch with.

My special thanks to Rashmi, who stood by me always during my bad and good times. Thanks to her and her beautiful smile which worked as strength for me to do this book.

Mohit Goel (Mogo), who converted my ideas into sketches. The graphic designer of my book.

I would like to express my gratitude to my publisher who encouraged me.

Last and not least: I beg forgiveness of all those who have been with me over the course of the years and whose names I have failed to mention.

With that, I hope you are ready to portray *Nothing For You My Dear!*

Adidas, Reid & Taylor, Allen Solley, Timex, Nike, John Players, UCB and Levis were some of the brands that Avinash was fond of all the time. His wardrobe overflowed with the newest products of these brands. Avinash's latest passion was a Honda's sports-bike.

His hit list included the ladies stuff, with jewellery topping it.

It was Avinash with his imposing six-foot frame, dressed in a grey Reid & Taylor suiting, a brand that he liked. Avinash was the kind of guy who actually got on your nerves in the very first meeting. His physical appearance was no less than that of a super-model, his way of dressing, his smartness and of course his intelligence attracted everyone around him.

But Avinash had stopped caring about his passions and desires long ago.

The reason?

Nobody knew.............till the day he visited **Sarika's Beauty Parlour - for Ladies only.**

9:00 AM (12 August 2008)

"Mom....Mom" shouted Avinash.

"Ya I am coming.....what happened?" replied Mrs. Jain from the kitchen.

"I am leaving for office, just check if the knot of the tie is alright"

"Office!! You are not going today. Didn't I tell you yesterday?"

"Mom, I am least concerned about that. Now will you come here or I should leave?"

"What is the problem beta? The girl is really good. Why don't you just see her once?" said Mrs Jain.

"Mom, I am not interested. I am concentrating on my career at the moment, let me first push up my bank balances" replied Avinash.

"You are 24 now. We will feel relaxed once we are over with our responsibilities son"

"Mom....I have not yet prepared myself for at. Please don't distract me on this issue" said Avinash sounding a little irritated.

"Neha, is very pretty and from a very good family", Mrs Jain tried to explain.

"Good. You see her and enjoy talking to her. Now please let me go to work." said Avinash, rather irritated by now.

"Beta, we like the girl. And we have already committed ourselves to her parents to meet us in the evening."

"I don't care." said Avinash in anger and walked off to the main door of the house.

"Is this the way to talk to your Mom?" she started crying.

"Oh Mom....please don't. I love you more than anything but please don't force me to marry"

"You don't love me. You are just concerned about your own life. We are not a part of it and you confirm it everyday. You are least bothered about our image. We have already asked them to come in the evening" said Mrs Jain, tears streaming down her face.

"Okay....stop crying. Okay I'll come a little early in the evening." said Avinash and started his bike.

"Make sure you come by five."

"Okay I'll come. And make sure that you won't ever repeat this sort of emotional blackmail."

Avinash nodded and went off to work.

Avinash, better known as Avi was a 24 year old - 6 feet tall - handsome guy. He had graduated two years back. Something had gone wrong during college days and that totally changed his life. A guy who never used to sit quiet for even a second was now very reserved. He had big groups of friends but today he didn't have even a one. He had loved playing pranks, he had many girlfriends, a great sense of humour, had loved adventures, and thrill, he had loved hanging out late at night. Life had been a romance. Today, his daily schedule included just three meals and office.

Mr and Mrs Jain were tense as to what the reason behind his changed behaviour could be.

"Why is he stressing himself? Is he not happy with his job?" Mrs Jain asked her husband.

"I don't know Sneha. He chose the job of his own choice. We made an offer to him to join the family business, he had said that he will join after 1-2 years of experience in the market. There is no financial problem either. He is medically fit, what could be the reason?" Mr Jain sounded worried.

"There is something which he is hiding from all of us, I am telling you" said Mrs Jain and started crying.

"Don't worry, don't worry. Everything will be fine." said Mr Jain.

"He is such a sweet boy. He loves us like anything but I don't know what the matter is, why he has started behaving like this? You know he is not even eating properly." said Mrs Jain, bursting into tears.

"Stop worrying Sneha. We will talk to him." said Mr Jain and held his wife close.

5:00 PM

"Welcome, Welcome......*ham log aapka hee intezar kar rahe the.*" said Mrs Jain to the Bhandaris. Mr and Mrs Bhandari (parents of Neha) were on their way from Ahmedabad to Kolkata. At the request of Mr Jain they had taken the tour via Jaipur.

"Please come in." Mr Jain escorted the guests to the drawing room.

"Please baithiye....." said Mr Jain.

"*Beta paani le aao.*" Mr Jain requested his daughter.

"*Aapko aane mei koi takleef to nai hui?*" asked Mrs Jain.

"No not at all. It was a comfortable journey. Air hostesses take good care of everything." said Mr Bhandari.

"Where's Neha? Didn't she come?" asked Mrs Jain.

"No, No she has come with us. But she'd be reaching in an hour. She forced us to drop her at the beauty parlour." smiled Mrs Bhandari.

"*Aajkal ke bacche bhi na!!*" said Mrs Jain.

"*Ab bas kya kahe. Zamaana hee badal gaya hai.* I never remember *kabhi makeup kiya ho.*" said Mrs Bhandari.

"Ya thats true. Maine to *apni shaadi mei bhi makeup nahi karaya tha.*" said Mrs Jain.

"Waise Neha is very pretty. *Hamare yaha to sabne photos dekhte hee haan kar diya tha.*" Mrs Jain said.

"Hmmm.....*aur Avinash Ji ke liye bhi kuch aisa hee hua.*" said Mr Bhandari.

"*Lijiye paani lijiye.*" Mr Jain offered water to everyone. "*Beta chaay-nashta le aao.*"

"Where's Avinash Ji by the way?" asked Mr Bhandari.

"He had some urgent work in office, must be coming in a few minutes." said Mr Jain.

"So he is totally into business now. That's great about this generation." Mr Bhandari said.

"Ya that's true. Avi is very sincere towards his work."

"Same is the case with Neha. She is always up with something or the other." said Mrs Bhandari.

"I am eagerly waiting for her to come." said Mrs Jain.

"How will she come here?" asked Mr Jain to Mr Bhandari.

"Her friend is going to drop her."

"*Kamaal karte hain aap. Ghar mei gaadi-driver hai aur aap.....*" said Mr Jain.

"Why not ask Avi to pick her up?" sugested Mrs Jain.

"Avinash Ji?" surprised Mr and Mrs Bhandari.

"Ya, it would be great" said Mr Jain.

"Sneha what's his new mobile number?"

"9720762538."

"Its ringing......Ya Avi beta where are you?" asked Mr Jain.

"Papa, I am on my way, reaching in fifteen minutes"

"Can you do me a favour?"

"Is this a thing to be asked Papa?"

"Can you please go to Sarika's Beauty Parlour in C-scheme to pick Mr & Mrs Bhandari's daughter up?" asked Mr Jain.

"What? Beauty Parlour!!! No Dad this would be impossible for me."

"Ya, Okay. Its on Prithviraj Road, opposite HDFC bank's ATM" said Mr Jain.

"Dad, I am not going. Why don't you send the driver?"

"Ya, good. Make sure that you don't get late. Neha must be waiting."

"Dad........."

"Ok beta, bye" said Mr Jain and rang off.

"He is such a sweet boy. One good quality of Avi is that he is very obedient" said Mr Jain.

"*Jab tak bachhe aate hain aap log ye lijiye.*", Mrs Jain offered snacks.

"*Arrey itna kuch banane ki kya zaroorat thi? Bhai ladki waale to ham hain aur khaatir-daari aap log kar rahe hain.*" said Mr Bhandari.

"*Agar ham log ye gap banaye rakhenge na to kabhi apni bahu ko apni beti nahi bána paayenge.*" said Mrs Jain.

"*Waise aapka to construction ka kaam hai na?*" asked Mr Bhandari.

"*Haan marble mining ka hai aur electronic goods ka distribution Rajasthan mein* we are planning to open a manufacturing unit in Madhya Pradesh with Avi."

And the conversation continued.

5:30 PM Sarika Beauty Parlour

Avinash reached the spot to pick his would-be wife up.

"Dad is really too much. Huh!! How am I going to identify her?" Avinash said to himself.

It was embarrassing for Avinash to get into a ladies beauty parlour. He had never touched cosmetics in his life and had never touched ornaments & jewellery. He waited patiently outside the parlour. Fifteen minutes passed and he couldn't see anyone coming out.

"Dad, have you informed Neha that I am waiting outside?" asked he.

"Beta, she is not carrying a cellphone. You go."

"Dad, you know I won't do that and that's for sure."

"Ya okay Beta. Now come soon, we all are waiting for both of you eagerly"

"Papa.....Papa....Listen"

Avinash was left with no option but to enter the parlour, which he hated. Inside he came across many things which he was allergic to.

Somehow he managed to trace down Neha Bhandari.

"Hi" said Avinash.

"Hi" said Neha, with her eyes down.

"Neha, I am Avinash, Avinash Jain. Dad had asked me to pick you up." he said.

"Pick me up!! Are you really going to pick me up?" said Neha, and smiled.

"Oh no no....I didn't mean that. Actually, the driver had gone somewhere and I was going this way....so"

"So....so you will pick me up!" she said and laughed.

Avinash too, smiled.

"*Ab uthao mujhe, papa ne kaha hai na?*" she said.

"*Oh ho....kya baat hai, aap to bahot sundar sharmate hain*" said Neha.

"Okay, I am sorry for that. Now, let's go" Avinash managed to say.

Neha seemed to be a talkitive girl. She didn't lose any opportunity to pull his leg.

"Neha, stop all this. I mean how can you talk to a person, whom you are meeting for the first time, like this" said Avinash irritated.

"Because I love you Avinash. And I am not meeting you for the first time, I met you the day when I saw your photographs, when I read about you, when mom and dad told me about you, that the day I met Avinash" she said, with moist eyes.

"See Neha, let me be very frank, I can't marry you."

For Neha it was difficult to digest. She was stunned. She kept gazing at Avinash. She had never expected this.

"Neha......it's not that you are not nice. But there is some other reason that I don't want to marry ever in life" said Avinash.

"What? What could be the reason Avinash?"

"Neha, you are a nice, intelligent and a beautiful girl, your parents, your family is also very nice. My parents have already accepted you as their daughter-in-law, I love my parents the most in the whole world and so I can't go against their decision." said Avinash.

"I am not getting you Avinash" said Neha in tears, streaming down her face.

"I won't be able to......you have to reject me in front of my parents." said Avinash, firmly.

"What's the reason Avinash? Is there some other girl in your life?"

"No"

"You didn't like me?" asked Neha.

"No....I like you but......."

"Please Avinash, it's about my life. Please tell me everything clearly. Please don't bring in suspenses.....please" Neha requested.

"I can't explain it to you."

"Wow!! Avinash! This is you, whom everybody was praising? I wonder how you have been successful in fooling people about yourself. I wonder how you have been the one who has been the leader of the pack throughout school and college life, I wonder how you have been the one considered very sensible and responsible. I wonder why I am sitting with a shit person like you." said Neha.

Avinash stood numb. He started trembling. Tears rolled down his face. "Do you want to know the reason Neha?" he asked.

Neha remained silent.

"Okay Neha then listen to it as it matters so much to you."

My Parent's second invention

However long we may live, we never forget the time when we were young. Memory is like a film which we alone can watch. For me, childhood was the best part of that film: time and again my thoughts return to my experiences, the innocence and mischief of that time, and the dreams and nightmares too.

It has now been 24 years since I came into the world, on 26 March 1984 in the Pink City of India. But strangely there's almost nothing that I do not remember. Things automatically twist to extremes whenever I am around and the same happened on the day I was born.

26 March was very unusual in Dadoo's nursing home, Jaipur. The air in the clinic was unusual; nurses were in a jolly mood, the sweepers were whistling while cleaning the floor, the peons were moving to the beat of the light music being played in the clinic. Dr. Dadoo went

crazy when saw his staff's behaviour in such an odd manner, "something has happened with them, crazy people" said he.

My father, granpa and granma were eagerly waiting for the good news. Arrangements for a grand get-together had already been made. "*Mr. Jain you have again become daddy of a beautiful healthy baby boy!!*" shouted Dr. Dadoo.

Tears rolled my Pa's eyes....he rushed into the room to meet the beautiful lady, yes I am talking about my mom. My dad kissed mumma and gave her a warm hug, all relatives then entered the room to congratulate her!! A grand party was thrown after thirty days to all relatives and friends of Daddy and Mummy to celebrate my birth.

Three months later we shifted from Jaipur, to the heart of the nation. Daddy was into the construction business, he was doing projects in the outskirts of the city. Shahdra, Noida and Ghaziabad were the areas under him for the construction of school buildings.

Mom used to be a bit disappointed as had to manage everything in the new city. A city culturally different. A city with diversified customs. We being from a Jain family had difficulties adjusting ourselves to the Punjabi's and Sindhi's around us.

My mom describes me as a very notorious and witty child. A child with chubby cheeks, mischievous brown eyes, and always the centre of attraction amongst the neighbors. I used to do a lot of irksome things which the neighbors were fed up of.

I used to look under the skirts of my female friends to find out if something's different!!-eh!!

Daily in the evening, Mom used to give us (me and bhayia) 2 rupees to play games at Jacob's Videogame Parlor. It became our habit to knock mom's door sharp at 5 for our daily allowance.

'JUNPO' was my player and 'ZEDD' was my bro's player. We used to fix 10 matches daily which used to end in about an hour.

"*You lost it Bhayia....*" I used to scream even if I had lost the match.

My naniji's arrival at our place in Delhi was the first incident of my life which tagged me as the most unpredictable child.

It was our summer holidays, bhayia and I were waiting eagerly for the clock to strike five. *"Mummy.....give us our money. Its five in the clock"* shouted I. But mom didn't entertain me, she was busy talking to ninja...eh....naniji.

It was really difficult for me to be patient as our gaming time was getting killed. I was a person who didn't sit idle for even a pico-second.

"Bhayia I know that mummy takes out money from her almirah. She is busy right now. Why to disturb her?" I whispered into bhayia's ears.

Bhayia always hides his light under the bushes. I guess he knew that taking out money from the cupboard without Mom's permission would definitely fetch me something disastrous. But he didn't stop me from doing that.

I picked up some currency notes and we went to the gamedrome.

Rahul bhayia, owner of the gamedrome was shocked to see Rs 2500 in my hands to play a set of scheduled games. He brought me back to our home and informed my mom about the matter.

"From where did you get the money??" asked mom.

I didn't answer.

"Avi from where did you get the money I am asking you the last time!"

Still I didn't answer.

Naniji came outside to see the matter and informed mumma that the amount has been taken from her purse. Mom lost control. Fumes fled from her head. Her heart seemed to stop.

She picked my cricket bat lying in the corridor when Naniji interrupted and asked mom to tackle the situation calmly.

Mom didn't say anything to me and took me in.

The next day Naniji left for Jaipur. The hot magma got the space to bulge out. I was thrashed hard!

It taught me a lesson not to pick anything from any place without the concerned person's permission. I resolved never to steal again.

My parents wanted me to be free from any kind of shackles, mentally or physically, and they wanted me to own the world. So obviously they taught me lessons, on all the times I committed mistake!!

Thank you tadpoles

Light-blue shirt, white shorts, white socks, sports shoes, burnt sienna colored bag on shoulders and a water bottle in hand was the attire I carried for the first day of my school.

After kindergarten, I was admitted to Apeejay School, Noida. Apeejay is a premier institution in Delhi. A hexagonal building, swimming pool, lush-green playgrounds, basketball courts, laboratories, hobby rooms, pond and a canteen made up the campus of the school.

Apeejay was the only built up structure in that part of Noida at that time. Barren landscape surrounded the boundary of the school, rough and ragged roads used to accompany me from Delhi till I reached the school.

Daily during the recess hour I used to play in the field which had a small pond. It had lots of frogs and tadpoles. I enjoyed playing near the pond.

Amongst our favorite games was pushing each other into the pond, making mud balls and targeting friends. Well, putting tadpoles into pockets of others was my favorite mischief.

Lenika, one of my classmate once got stuck with us boys, she joined our pranks and even enjoyed herself. She messed up my hair and poured wet mud on me. Ankit and Lokesh joined her. Both of them gripped my hands hard while Lenika tore my shirt and put mud into my vest. I felt as if I was being gangraped.

I was greatly embarrassed. To take revenge; I picked three-four tadpoles, pulled Lenika's top and threw them in. She went crazy and started screaming madly, she jumped here and there as if she had the shoes with spring under them. The tadpoles must be dancing inside.....eh!!

I went mad laughing at her. "*Hey Lenika, I didn't know you dance so well!*"

She started crying and ran into the school building straight to the staff room to complain about me.

"Ma'am Avinash pulled my top and threw tadpoles inside." she cried.

I could easily sense of what was going to happen to me in the next couple of minutes.

The class coordinator harshly punished me. I had thought that crime committed for self-defense is non-punishable!

I was expected to say sorry, which I didn't. The ultimate solution left with her was to hit me hard with a ruler. *One...two...three...four....* She kept on hitting me and I stood like a zombie but tears were rolling down my face.

When I was about to get the fifth one, Lenika interrupted, "Ma'am, please don't hit him anymore, please don't hit him", she pleaded with her to forgive me.

I was taken aback. My inner soul cursed me for hurting such an innocent girl. Now I did not feel comfortable to have even an eye-contact with her. I was ashamed of myself.

"It is your first and last warning Avinash! Next time if you are found doing any of such thing, I am going to call your parents." shouted Hitler.

I remained silent.

Well, I believed that we must have a positive attitude towards visualizing things. All that happens is for the good of us.

I am thankful to god that I put the tadpoles in her top in my childhood at an age when we don't have physical differences. Had I done the same at this age, people would have shot me dead!!

Next day, again during the recess we encountered each other near the pond. I was not yet ready to face her, so had to change my place, I went to the main field where I used to climb up and down the network of poles.

It feels very unusual if everything goes as per the expectations and plans. I made my den at the out field where there were swings, slide and such other stuff.

I was enjoying hanging upside-down to pretend being part of the *Vikram-Betaal* duo. But all of a sudden I became a hilarious *betaal*. After climbing up the 5 mtr high pole, as I let myself free to hang upside down, my trousers got stuck into a screw. I was struck with wardrobe malnutrition. My trousers were completely torn. I lost my balance and fell on to the ground.

I heard hearty laughter; it seemed very familiar, I was feeling ashamed as my underpants were visible.

"Hey white panty should I help you?" giggled Lenika.

I didn't look at her.

"Hey, you are fairer than me" she said.

It was very embarrassing, I mean it is bad to face someone of the opposite sex when you are in such a condition. Facing Lenika in such a pathetic state was beyond my wildest imagination.

7

She helped me to arrange myself. She couldn't control her laughing. I felt like committing suicide. I ran to the bathroom to hide from everybody.

From that very moment she started teasing me about it. I felt bad about the incident and didn't like the way she laughed at me. It became our daily routine to fight on some issues or other file complaints against each other and then feel sorry.

I remember when I had completed 9 orbits around the sun (in the year 1993), mom told me that soon we were to shift to Jaipur, the place where I was born. Daddy got construction projects in Kukas Industrial Area, 20kms from Jaipur main city. I was very happy and excited about the new home and wanted to leave as early as possible.

I got a small farewell from my classmates in Apeejay, Noida.

Everybody seemed to be unhappy about my departure. Surely they were going to miss me a lot!!! I can still recall the faces of my class-fellows, especially Lenika. Tears were rolling down her cute face, it seemed they were trying to follow me.

May be this was my perception, but I don't know why it felt like an emotional attachment.

Tears made her cheeks shine as if they have been rubbed with diamonds.

It pinched like safety pins inserted into the valves of my heart. I guess I had a soft corner for her. I just didn't know why I was feeling bad?

I hugged all my friends, even Lenika and then left the city forever.

I missed them all.

We then shifted to Jaipur.

You know Neha, Jaipur is a wonderful city to live in. It has a royal touch. Amber Fort, Nahargarh Fort, Jaigarh Fort, Moti Doongri Fort, Hawa Mahal, Jantar Mantar, City Palace, Jal Mahal, Samod Palace are some of the amazing architectural sites of the ancient and the Mughal times which take you back to the golden days of our ancestors. The ambience of the forts makes you feel romantic.

I can now say that Jaipur is my city. You can consider it the best residential city of India. It is not one of those hip cities like Delhi, Mumbai or Bangaluru but its simple and unique in its own way. The royal heritage of the city automatically entraps our attention.

I believe that every person born in this world must visit this city at least once.

I was admitted in standard four at Children's Academy, an ICSE board school, which was right in front of our home.

I used to be a very shy guy and avoided female company. There is an incident which took place during the examination and which is worth telling. Mrs. Saxena, the examination controller, had come on a visit for inspection.

It was our English paper and there were certain words whose meanings were to be written. I feel sorry when it comes to vocabulary and grammar, right from my childhood. I find grammar is some bull-shit for *crammers*! Well, I didn't know any of the meanings in the question paper. Saxena Ma'am tried to prompt me with the point of her sandals, but I didn't react. It was beyond me to see that she wanted me to copy the answers from my neighbor's answer sheet. And unfortunately all my neighbors were girls, so it became impossible for me to peep into their sheets and copy.

The result was that everyone passed except me. I had been so stupid! Neha smiled at this.

"Ya, I was that shy" said Avinash.

"Its hard to believe that a guy who fell in love in pre-primary years of his life was now shy of talking to girls" said Neha.

"Neha, I am telling you the truth. I have never talked about my life to anyone. I am telling you because it's related to our future." said Avinash.

"Avinash, please proceed. I want to know what could be the reason that you like me but can't marry me." said Neha, putting her hand on Avinash's.

Diwali
"Bash"

It was our Dipawali vacations. Dipawali is the time which all of us eagerly wait for. We get ample time to decorate the house, meet relatives and friends, buy new clothes, eat sweets and the year long awaited dry fruits.

And on top of everything, lighting up crackers is heartily celebrated. Cock Brand and Anil Fireworks were amongst my favorites.

A budget of rupees three thousand was sanctioned by the Finance Ministry at home. Actually in our home all the ministries i.e. the Finance Ministry, the Home Ministry, the Information & Broadcasting Ministry were all headed by one single supreme power. And I am sure that you know who can it be? Because this is *Kahani Ghar Ghar Ki*. Three cheers for Ekta Maa!!!

Well, Bhayia and I were firework freaks. Rockets, jameen-chakkars, shooting stars, flowerpots, ten-thousand-ladi-bombs, laxmi bombs, sootli bombs and even the wimpy phuljhadi- we loved them all.

Nothing thrilled me and bhayia more than strutting down to the brightly decorated stalls on the Hawa Mahal road to discuss the merits of Anil brand versus cock brand with the shopkeepers who sold them. It used to be great fun deciding what to buy – the very big silver-and-red cascade rockets with bollywood hot babes on the box, or the golden-green paper covered aerial fireworks? The dotted, glittering pencils or the striped chakrees?

And in the end a number of fireworks including all our favourites were procured for us.

Bhayia, my elder brother, is three and a half years elder than me. He is a very charming personality. Lots of ideas keep pumping his mind every milli-second. He has a great sense of humor. He is very good at modifying the lyrics of any song in keeping with the situation.

Well Neha, let me not divert you from the celebration of Diwali. Crackers commonly available in the market have some specified norms for controlled sound level, and so the manufacturers obey the restrictions. To me it was not interesting at all. I wonder how people enjoy themselves on such bull-shit sound quality of the crackers. I wanted the crackers whose sound could be heard till a range of kilometers. But there was no availability of fireworks as per my choice. I decided to make a huge bomb on my own. For this surely I needed Bhayia's help.

We jotted down the ingredients required.

I started piling up the gunpowder from the diffused bombs. I un-foiled around 150 foil bombs to collect *barood*, the explosive material inside. The heap of the IEP ie: Intensive Explosive Powder as I called it), was fair enough to make an explosion which could be heard up to several thousand meters. The total weight of the gunpowder must have been around 700grams. I was damn excited about the experiment I was going to conduct.

Bhayia was ready with the lit match-stick to inaugurate the IEP Bomb. "Avi get aside! I am throwing the matchstick..." he yelled.

The lit matchstick slipped from his grip and fell straight into the heap without even giving me a second's time to move.

Booooommmmm......!!!!!

"*Aaaaaaaaaaa.......Mummmmmmaaaaaa!!!*", I screamed at the top of my voice.

I was burnt badly.

"Oh no...." said Neha and closed her eyes tightly, feeling the pain.

Bhayia rushed me into the bathroom and quickly sat me down under the cold water tap.

"*Please save me bhayia I don't want to die!*"

"*I am not able to see bhayia*", I cried.

"*Avi nothing's gonna happen to you, believe me!*", he held my hand.

After being in cold water for more than ten minutes, Bhayia applied Colgate toothpaste all over my body, to prevent me from the pains of burn. Actually the paste works as ointment and prevents the swelling after burns.

It was his presence of mind that saved me from the intense pains.

The nearest hospital was around 800 meters from our place. As nobody was at home, Bhayia took me to the hospital all by himself lifting me up in his arms till the Shah Hospital.

The doctor was shocked to see me in that condition. I was completely burnt. My eyebrows, eyelashes, hair all gone. The skin of the whole body was badly burnt.

Dr. Shah made an urgent call to all his team members and instructed them to give me the first aid. I was rushed to the operation theatre. By the time I was getting first aid, mom reached. It was fairly difficult for mom to see me in such a condition.

"He has got severe burns Mrs. Jain, 67% of the tissues are damaged.

I guess he needs to undergo plastic surgery!", said Dr. Shah in a sympathetic voice.

Mom was unable to utter a single word, she could not decide what to do.

Daddy was out of station for some business deal.

By 10:00 in the evening all our family members collected at the hospital. With concern of everybody mom decided to allow the operation for plastic surgery. A team of specialists including surgeons, dermatologists, physicians, cardiologists was called from SMS Hospital and Durlabhji Hospital. These are the most advanced and reputed hospitals of Jaipur. The surgery took about hundred and forty minutes. It was all greatly done, the doctors came out with confident gestures. It gave an immense pleasure to all our relatives who were waiting outside the OT.

"Your Child is absolutely OK," said one of the surgeon before anybody could ask something.

"Can I see him?" cried mom.

"Can I meet Bhayia, Sir?" enquired my sis, Tinni in a hushed voice.

"No. He is to be kept under vigilance for the next 3 hours. After that you can't just meet him but take him home."

"Now please stop worrying Mrs. Jain," said Dr. Shah very supportively.

"By the way your child is amazing Mrs. Jain. He was very cooperative. It really helped us in doing the surgery," said Dr. Shah.

Mom was speechless. She was dying to meet me, to touch me and take me back home.

Everybody could be seen at the corridor except my bhayia. Like *Paarvati* and *Tulsi* of Ekta Kapoor's disgusting episodes, Bhayia was crying like hell as he felt that it was his fault and he was to be blamed totally for my condition.

But it was not at all his mistake, it was just by chance that it happened. The Doctor even said that if Bhayia would not have given me first aid, it would have been a complicated surgery.

Well, finally I was brought back home.

I was recommended complete bed-rest for three months. I was not allowed to see the mirror. Mom used to cover my face with a thin cotton cloth whenever somebody visited to see me. My earlier pictures and the pictures of that time were very well able to indicate the difference between white and black races of America. I looked like an Egyptian mummy, a thousand years old.

It took me more than six months to recover. Life came back on the normal track. I started going back to school.

From that very incident I learned that there is no substitute to strong will power.

Neha, please stop feeling bad about it because there is much more in my life.

School,
Cool & Sonal

After one year of hostel life in GDBMS (Ghanshyam Das Birla Memorial School), Ranikhet, I returned and got admission in MPS (Mahaveer Public School), Jaipur. I was in seventh standard. The journey of one year's hostel life in Ranikhet was an experience of its own kind. Ranikhet is a hill station and cantonment town in the Almora district in the state of Uttrakhand. It is the home of the Kumaon Regiment (KRC) and Naga Regiment and is maintained by the Indian Army.

It is at an altitude of 1869 metres above sea level and within sight of the western peak of the Himalayas. This town's history has a wonderful story. Ranikhet got its name from a local legend, Raja Sudhardev, who won the heart of his queen, Rani Padmini, who subsequently chose this area for her residence and thus named it as Ranikhet. This place becomes very cold in winters and remains moderate in summers. A large variety of flora and fauna is seen. I remember when we used to come up to our school in Ranikhet from Kathgodam (nearest railway station), we used to see pine, oak and deodar trees in un-ending number. It offered a beautiful sight.

We had a very strict routine to be followed. There were morning and evening PT session, which I used to hate the most. I considered it to be a girl's job, just like aerobics. But now that I am grown up, I realize the importance of those PT sessions. We used to have even morning and evening prayers. In the morning we were supposed to pray on our own and in the evening we had to assemble for a prayer to *Surya Deva*. From eight in the morning to two in the afternoon we had to be in the academic block for our regular classes. Sanskrit was the subject I never wanted to study.

Well, after the classes, we were given thirty minutes to change and have our meal. After that we had to go to the hobby hall, to somehow kill one hour. Everything was forced on us. It was all very mechanical. After the hobby hour, we had to attend lectures on morality in the academic block again. Damn boring they used to be.

At about five in the evening we finally got free this was followed by a ten minute tea break and we had to rush to the respective sport field to join our respective teams. I took part in Taekwando and Table Tennis. Our Taekwando coach was a very large built man. I never attempted to make an eye contact with him. He can be compared to the present "Khali". I won't be surprised if somebody tells me that he was Khali's father!

We had to make sounds like Hoo, Haa, liaa, haa while practising the punches and kicks. I enjoyed this hour. Again, late in the evening, the robotic activities started. Fixed time to watch T.V, fixed time to talk to friends, fixed time to eat dinner and a fixed time to go to bed. I never liked the way we were treated. You can portray my image as that of Ishaan in *Taare Zameen Par*, the only difference was that I was admitted to hostel voluntarily.

During the winters I faced severe cold. The temperature was sub zero. My fingers was swollen because of chillblain, my eyes bulged ...... Chillblain is an affliction in which the body parts which are exposed to the cold air are inflamed and start itching. I had to give my final exams as verbally as I could not write.

Mom and Dad got me back to Jaipur and admitted me to MPS.

The only good part of the hostel life was that it made me independent. It helped me in improving my decision making ability, it helped me in learning the tactics to face difficulties confidently. I was happy to be back home.

I entered this school (MPS) in seventh standard. It was the senior most class in the school. The school was new built and every year one more class was added, we were always the seniors. Lucky me!!

I always enjoyed the affection of my teachers. I was not amongst the dunces. I never got a bad certificate, though I was among the most mischievous students. There was nothing wicked left that I had not done myself or helped my friends to do. *Great people do common things uncommonly* was deeply engraved in my mind. I always used to plan my escape before doing anything wrong. I was never caught. My teachers had a fantastic impression of me.

I was selected as the House Captain as soon as I got into class IX for my enthusiasm and dynamism. We had four houses in school: Neelkanth the blue one. Bulbul – the reds, Hans – the yellows and Mayur – the greens. I was in Neelkanth. All the houses had an equal number of students, but there was always a race for our house and Bulbul house while filling up the priority column during admissions.

The day I was selected as the house captain, I made the resolution that it was going to get the Best House trophy. I remember my weekly interactions with the students of my house. I used to motivate and encourage them for participation. Daily after the assembly, we had a zero hour. The zero hour was earmarked for extra curricular activities. We had Judo, Vocal Music, Dramatics, Dance, Instrumental Music, Drawing, etc. I opted for Dramatics. I had written many short plays and directed them. Three of the very popular ones were "The Mango Man", "Shrimaan Musa" and "Telephone Ki Ghanti". Students and teachers loved the way I presented my ideas. All the plays were comic, but had some message at the end.

Being the script writer and director, I always took the leading role and presented myself to the best. I enjoyed the part when I used to select the characters for my script. The most beautiful looking girl used to become my wife always. I don't know what thralls I used to get by doing that but I admit that I was always biased on that account, though I was very shy of talking to anyone of the opposite sex. I don't remember that I ever initiated a talk with some girl. It was only during the plays or some activity in college that I used to interact with them.

Jennisha, Akanksha, Surbhi and Sonal were the hot-shots of our school. The boys were *lattu* on them. And I am a boy! Ya, I wanted them all to be my closest friends or girlfriends. I didn't have a clear concept the difference between a good female friend and a girl friend. But now I know Neha.

So, I used to select someone from them, for the role of my wife in the plays. Jennisha was my wife in "The Mango Man", Akanksha became my wife for "Shriman Musa" and Surbhi in "Telephone Ki Ghanti". Sonal never got the opportunity. I always assigned her the job of narrator. I liked her voice very much. She never liked it. She wanted to be in, she requested me many times but unfortunately I could never give her the chance to be my wife, which I had always wanted to. Please don't mind but it's true.

My skits used to mesmerize the audience. I became a real superstar in school. The teachers from all the wings (senior, junior and primary) started knowing me, I became *Krishh* for my juniors. That was the time when Datt ma'am (Principal) helped me to channelize my energy. She presented me with maximum opportunities. I was sent to different schools for the inter-school competitions. I bagged many prizes. Debates, extempore, essay writing, quiz, JAM sessions, advertisement making, skit competition, I got plenty of awards in all the categories.

And all my awards were presented to me in the school assembly. I was greatly honored on all occasions I won in the competitions but Datt Ma'am never let me day-dream and feel over-confident about my achievements.

She used to say "Success comes with great responsibilities. You must not forget the people, the time when you were preparing for success", her words inspired me to constantly work hard for next ventures ahead but with a *ground-to-earth* attitude.

I must tell you about my first experience of giving an extempore speech. There was an intra-school extempore competition. I never wanted to participate in it because speaking something on the spot was like a Van-Vilder kind of nightmare to me. I had never done it before. But the expectations of my teachers and my juniors made me participate. Very confidently I got my name registered and sat amongst the reserved seats of participants. I was very nervous. I could feel the blop-blop of my heart on my blazer.

Sangeeta Ma'am introduced the judges and announced the rules and judging criteria of the competition. I was not able to resist that, I closed my eyes and started praying to god for help. "Let us give a huge round of applause for our first participant, Avinash Jain" she announced.

First!!! God damn.... I had registered last. How could that happen? Was that for what I prayed to god for!! Oh no....oh no...!! I froze.

"You will do wonders. I know", Principal ma'am wished me.

Somehow I managed to move up to the stage, to the podium. I picked up the slip from the box, with my hands trembling, as if I was standing on a naked electric wire. I opened the slip and read the topic aloud as instructed, "It is nice to be important but it is more important to be nice".

As soon as I finished reading the topic, one of the judges struck the buzzer to start the time. Damn goodness! the time started and I had not understood the topic yet. But then without a giving a thought to it I just started speaking. The first line with which I started was "Success comes with great responsibilities. You must not forget the people, the time when you were preparing for success" I don't know how it appeared in my mind. And then I mentioned the names of Lord Mahaveer, Ashoka the Great, Mughal Baadshah Akbar, Abraham Lincoln, Mahatma Gandhi, Adolf Hitler and even the corporate personalities like Ratan Tata, GD Birla, Narayanmurthi, Rishabh Bajaj, Henry Ford I mentioned some of their great works and related them with their social life. After continuously speaking for two minutes I actually realized what the topic demands me to say. And then I focused upon the importance of being nice. I ended with "If you want that people should remember you forever than prove your importance while being nice. Thank You". And the hall roared with clapping.

"Very well said" said Kiran Ma'am.

"Ma'am, I don't know what I spoke" I replied and moved to my seat.

The competition continued with fourteen more participants. A few of them didn't say anything. They just came to the stage, showed their faces to the audience and went away. Whenever such a thing happened, I used to say to myself "Had this topic been given to me, I would have done wonders". But no issues as I had already spoken quite well.

After listening to everyone, I was sure that one the three positions would definitely be mine. A fifteen minute break was given for the evaluation of the results. We were busy calculating the ranks ourselves. *"Mera to bekaar tha, but you were great"* said one the participants. *"Main to haar gaya, kuch samajh hee nai aa raha tha kya bolu"* said Shekhar. "My topic was very difficult" and it went on.

I wonder what pleasure people feel by making such statements. I was silent and waiting impatiently for the results. Well, the break got over, I held my breath to listen to the names of the winners.

"On third position is........Manas Gupta" Sangeeta ma'am announced. We all clapped till Manas reached the stage. Now, for the second position I was expecting my name.

"On second position is......any guesses??"

Different-different names were being shouted by the audience. Neelkanth House students were shouting my name. "Well, the second position goes to Ankit Vyas".

As soon as ma'am announced Ankit's name, my house's students lifted me on their shoulders to celebrate my victory.

"Boys and girls lets give a big round of applause for Avinash Jain on the first position" she exclaimed. This was unexpected of me and totally as per the expectaions of my colleagues, juniors and teachers. I didn't know that I spoke so well. The judges appreciated the content I had spoken. "You have the potential to become a great orator my child" one of the judges said patting my back.

It boosted my confidence greatly. I was then able to overcome the stage fright. It is just the matter of time. Once you are on stage and start your delivery, everything appears to be very normal. Just initiate and then have wonders lying for you.

I created history in the school by bagging prizes in series. But I failed on the part of team work, because it had become a one man show. And obviously the house trophy couldn't be won just by counting on my credits. Three years of my House-Captaincy and I was not able to get the House trophy. I changed my strategy and plan of action. My modus operandi was to focus on team participations. And so we diverted to the sports and athletics.

The Intra-school football tournament was one of the most popular mega events in the arena of sports in our school. Over ten days of excitement and thrill marked the enthusiastic start of it. It had four teams from the four houses. First three days the teams played practice matches with the other three. From the fourth day started the race for raising the points and moving to the next rounds. Mayur House was knocked out first. Then the semifinals was played between Hans, Neelkanths and Bulbuls. We gave a marvelous performance and entered the finals with highest points. Bulbuls followed us.

The tenth day was the final match. It was a celebration in colors and music. A team of students from the Instrumental Music Hobby group gave a sensational performance prior to the final. Hundreds of Neelkanth fans erupted in joy as Neelkanth's captain Deepankar Sharma entered in the ground with his team. Students cheered for both the teams as we paraded through the green room to the ground. Our team was dressed in blue t-shirt and white shorts and the BulBuls were in red and white. The players of both the teams were all set for the final show.

The sports coach of our school was the referee for the match. The players from both the teams shook hands and promised fair play. We took our positions. I was in the centre mid-field. The referee whistled to mark to start of the match.

The match started.

The ball was kicked by Akash of Bulbuls in our court. With the fullest of the energy the Bulbuls attacked. Our defenders gave a good fight and broke all their attempts. We were always successful in returning the ball to the other half of the court. And it carried on. But we were not able to show our best game, unlike the previous editions of our performance in the tournament.

After forty five minutes when the first half was over, the scoreboard showed 1-0.

We were losing!!

After the drinks break, the match began with the referee's whistle. We returned to the court with changed strategy. A strategy which had never been observed in any of the soccer matches before, in the history of soccer. We had changed the positions of all our players. The defenders took charge of the attacking positions and vice-versa. So, I was now at the defending end. Nobody in the field was able to judge what we were up to.

The struggle of getting back into the match started. The ball passed, this time it was with our men. Deepankar didn't let the Bulbuls touch the ball. And the ball kept on rolling within our team. Thirty minutes passed and the scoreboard didn't show a rise in the score any of the teams. In the later part of the game, we mounted pressure on them, by frequent attacks.

The breakthrough came late in the game with Deepankar's goal at the 84-minute mark. Neelkanth supporters jumped in excitement. The audience celebrated the effort. The match had approached an exciting climax.

Now, a tie was not acceptable to us, especially when the opponents were Bulbuls. We were moving ahead for a second goal. The last few minutes were getting crucial.

Deepankar moved speedily towards their goal post and gave a skillful kick. The ball took flight aiming towards their goal. But it missed the post. The goalie of their team quickly kicked the ball, which directly landed into our side. At the defending end was the goalie and I. In the entire match I had not contributed much. So, now it was my turn to show them what students of Neelkanth house were like.

Shekhar, who was forward attacker of their team, kicked the ball straight towards our goal with maximum energy. I was the one standing in front of our goal post, in support of our goalie. The ball was approaching like a fire-ball. I turned back, faced my goalie. All were stunned to see what I was doing. I somersaulted into the air, stretching my legs to the fullest.

This is called a Banana Kick in soccer. The players of both the teams got stuck at their respective positions, seeing the stunt I had given. The spectators gaped open. The commentator stopped commenting.

I leapt into the air and kicked back with full energy.

I missed the ball!! It went straight into our goal post, which our goalie was not able to stop.

I fell back upside down on the ground. I had hurt my knees and ankle. My shorts tore from the button in the front to the elastic on waist at the back. My underwear was visible, clearly visible.

The score changed to 2-1, in the last thirty seconds of the match. We lost!!

The players of our team gathered around me to celebrate! Our captain Deepankar was the first to kick my bottom. "What was that?" he shouted, but laughed at the very next instant. He had his eyes on my undies…!!

None the players of our team were regretted losing the match, the Bulbuls were not celebrating their win either. Everyone was enjoying the scene I had created, more.

Within a few seconds I was surrounded by a group of girls. I could spot Sonal and Akanksha heading the *jhund* of chicks. I tried to escape but I couldn't run as my shorts were badly torn.

"*Kya chikni taange hain*" Sonal said.

That was humiliating I could bury myself in. I tried to cover my thighs from the flaps of the torn short. I couldn't do it properly. I wished to get buried into the ground. I looked at Akanksha, I was expecting her help to get me away from the scene.

"Wow!" she exclaimed, she bit her lower lip and winked. That was the naughtiest action she had ever tried in front of me.

"Please let me go, Akanksha please" I requested.

"Only on one condition sexy" Sonal interrupted.

"I agree to all your conditions, now let me go". More students had gathered around, as if I was enacting some *Nukkad Naatak*.

"No, first listen to it." she demanded.

"Please proceed." I said. I had no other option.

"I am not going to be the narrator in your next play. I want to be in it."

My heart zoomed. I smiled and nodded. I was then allowed to go. I heard a lot of comments from the students who had gathered around me, when I was rushing towards the green room.

Quickly I ran away and disappeared from the scene.

As the days passed, Sonal and I became good friends. She used to try weird pranks on me, which, most of the times I managed to stay clear of.

I remember one very funny incident which happened because of her. It was our computer class. In our school we had to take off our footwear before entering the computer laboratory. This was done to prevent the piling of the dust on the carpet.

Sonal had some mischief brewing. Akanksha always helped her. This was their daily routine. I guess they used to do homework on this to get such new-new ideas.

She poured fevicol into my shoes and silently entered the lab. With a very innocent face she came and sat by me. "Late again" I commented.

"I was waiting for Akanksha. She had gone to the loo."

The conversation continued till the class got over. We didn't make any of the programs we were assigned. I copied it from the other students and we presented them well. We were allowed to leave the lab in the order of our class roll numbers. So, I left before her. I put on my shoes and waited for her to come.

When she came, she looked at my feet with an open mouth. "Are these your shoes?"

"Ya….why?" I was confused.

"Oh Shit!!!" she said.

She had poured the fevicol in the computer science teacher's shoe. She always landed up in *ajeeb-o-gareeb* situations.

Miss. Ajeeb I started calling her. And she gave me the title of Mr. Ajeeb. Sonal when first titled me as Mr. Ajeeb, I wished our titles to change from **Mr. & Miss.** Ajeeb to **Mr. & Mrs.** Ajeeb.

Ya, I had a crush on my Miss Ajeeb.

But I didn't ever disclose my feelings out of a fear which all boys under the blue sky have. What if she doesn't like it? What if she takes it the other way? I feared of loosing her.

I was waiting for Deepak to come. Oops! How did I forget to tell you about Deepak. Deepak is a person whom I can trust blindly. We became friends when we were in eighth class. The four years in school were great fun with him. We were partners in all the pranks we planned. We bunked class, we studied together, we even took punishments together. He is a very cheerful chap and one who has survived all my deadliest pranks. I feel proud in taking the credit of getting him thrashed by almost all the chicks of our school. Poor fellow! But I liked our friendship.

So, I was waiting for him to come. I was standing all by myself in the parking lot. The parking lot was our favorite den. It was the place where we used to decide how to spend the day. The tuitions, the evening hang-outs, girls were all discussed here. All this happened very easily because the place was hardly visited by the teachers.

I was lost in my thoughts when I saw Sonal and Akanksha coming towards the parking lot. They were having some kinda girly gossip in typical girly style.

I was watching her for ten minutes, I could make out that they wanted to get noticed. Finally, after their long discussion, Sonal headed towards me. My heartbeat accelerated immediately. I started feeling nervous though there was no apparent reason.

"Hi!" she smiled.

I was dumb.

"How come *Baadshah* is sitting alone today? *Aaj aapki praja nai hai aapke saath?*" she commented.

"I am waiting for Deepak. It is very late, so the others have gone" I explained the reason why the *Praja* was not around.

"Well, that is great." she said.

"What is so great about it Ms. Ajeeb?"

"That I found you alone. Avi, I need to tell you something." she said softly.

I looked at her stonily.

"Avi, a girl likes you." she said in a low voice.

"Oh! Just one girl, I thought there are many." I interrupted.

"You can never be serious" she said, annoyed.

I had been so stupid at times Neha. I never realized the sentiments of the girl. Well, when a girl wants you to be serious there is something she wants to share with only you. I knew this very well but I couldn't trust Ms. Ajeeb. She has been playing a lot of pranks with me almost all the times she got a chance. And Akanksha always supported her for that.

"I was just kidding. You tell me." I regretted.

"You keep on kidding Okay" she got irritated. "I am leaving now." she added.

"Sorry dear. Please…" I implored.

She closed her eyes. She was trying to get over her irritation.

"Avi, a girl likes you." she started.

Now, I listened to her seriously. I was silent.

"She comes to our tuition class." she paused.

I don't know why girls tell only half the story. Don't mind Neha but most of them love playing mind games and it is truly said that even the one who has created them cannot judge what's going on their minds. And I believe that is the thing which we guys are crazy about. Girls are so innocent and beautiful in their own ways.

"Avi, she is in our batch" she hinted. Sonal expected me to guess the name. My mind scanned all the chicks in our batch Sonal was talking about. My brain started rolling out the names of the girls who could have liked me. Since I thought it could be just anyone, I couldn't really make out. I looked puzzled.

"Her name doesn't starts with M" she said. She helped me in filtering the names.

The absence of letter M in the initials frightened me. There were only four girls in our batch, two of whose names started with M and the other two were Akanksha and Sonal. Akanksha could never be the one. She is my closest female friend and if there was something she would have definitely told me directly. Then was it Sonal?

"Now tell me, who gave you this DARE?" I asked bluntly.

Girls and Guys are crazy about playing Truth & Dare. I find no interest in it. Who the hell cares about the personal life of others and nobody has time to listen to the truths voiced by other people. I just hated the game and that was why I asked her bluntly.

"Avi, I am serious. There is no Truth & Dare kind of thing." she insisted.

I went quiet.

I could see Akanksha standing behind Sonal. She had eyes on us but pretended that she was busy with something else.

"Akanksha?" I asked, knowing that she was not. Actually, the situation was getting difficult for me. I had never faced a proposal yet. So, I was a bit shy and nervous even. I was excited but nervousness dominated.

"No. Not Akanksha" she replied.

"Oh! You Miss Ajeeb?" I laughed. I thought it would divert the thing.

But her face tensed. Her eyes went wet. And slowly a drop of tear emerged. It first sat on her lower eyelash, rested for a moment and then slipped down. Gradually it came down her chubby cheeks.

Oh God! I had made her cry. It is really difficult for me to face a girl who is crying. It is so emotional. Whenever it happens, my heart melts and I find hugging, the best remedy for it. But in this case I couldn't do that, as we were standing inside the school campus. She sat sobbing for a while. I tried comforting her.

Somehow I had managed to pep her up.

"Sonal, I am sorry. Please don't cry" I said. I was on the urge of tears myself.

"This is not the right place to talk about this" I said, "let me drop you at your home, I will call you up in the evening" I added.

She didn't say anything and ran away. She was in tears. I just stood there, not knowing what to do.

In the evening I called her up but she didn't receive my call. In just a few hours everything changed. The sweet memories of tuition classes, school, the pranks which we played on each other, the time which we had spent together, all vaporized. It seemed as if I had entered a different world. She didn't talk to me for the whole of next week. The week then turned to a month and month to months.

Deepak, Akanksha and Nischay used to curse me about the way I had responded. They made me realize my stupidity. "You should have handled the situation very calmly and sensibly, you ass." Nischay shouted.

"You must say sorry and call her" said Deepak.

"Deepak, I have called her many times but she didn't take my call." I said.

"When it was your fault you don't need to count the number of times you called her." Deepak fired another salvo at me.

"*Ab apni ego side rakh aur usse baat kar.*" ordered Nischay and passed me his cell phone.

"*Meri ego*!! Yaar, what's my fault?"

"This is what ego is. Stop making calculations about your fault. Call her right now." he ordered.

I called but there was no response. "Now tell me whose ego is this? Nischay, why don't you guys understand?" I shouted in irritation.

"Either you go and talk to her or stop talking to me."

"Now what's that rubbish? Okay, I'll talk to her" I agreed.

I decided to face her.

The day finally came. It was the Diwali fete at the school. I had decided to talk to her and clear the issue. I wanted to tell her that I liked her too. I wanted to tell her that I was feeling sorry about that day. I wanted her to be mine.

But it is not easy to say all these things to a girl whom you really like. For me it was nearly impossible. To overcome the fear, Deepak and I used to practice what I was supposed to tell her on the final day. I remember, Deepak used to take on the role of Sonal and we practised the proposing sessions. Many a times those sessions lasted with a tight slap on my face. It happened so because I had asked him to react in the worst way he could. I did it because in this case I didn't want to take a chance. We are always ready to face the good that happens but I wanted to be prepared for the worst.

So, on the final day when we all met at Diwali fete, I gathered full of my courage to speak to her. It had been around two and half a months since we had not talked to each other, so I felt very uncomfortable in facing her.

Sonal was looking gorgeous that day. She had to be as I had chosen her to be my love. She was wearing a cut-sleeve green top, brown spaghetti and black jeans. She had folded the legs of her jeans three-four inch upwards. She wore dark green footwear through which her toes were visible. She had applied maroon nail-print. She even got a *mehandi* tattoo imprinted on her left arm. She was wearing a rose fragrance. I loved the way she dressed. I loved the way she was. I loved her simplicity and extreme innocence.

Deepak, Akanksha, Sonal, Nischay, Ani, Tina and I were standing in a circle. All were busy talking about beautifully organized fete. They were talking about the stalls, the surprise prizes, etc. I was lost in my own thoughts. Even Sonal didn't participate in the discussion.

After a couple of minutes, Akanksha, Tina and Nischay left. Deepak and Ani also made some excuse and moved on. They disappeared one after another. I was left alone so that I could talk to her. I looked at her, trying to make an attempt to start. No matter how brave you are, it all fails when one has to propose to a girl.

"I understand Avi" said Neha.

"Hi" I said.

"Hello" she replied. I didn't know how to go beyond the *hi* and *hello-ing*. I felt a tinge of regret at the rift that had developed between us.

"Isn't the fete great?" I said to kill the silence and nervousness dawn inside me.

"Ya it is. And your jacket is looking great too." she said.

"Just the jacket!!" I said to myself.

"Thanks" I said, "Bhaiya had gifted it to me." I added.

"So, how are you? Still insincere?" she taunted.

I didn't say anything.

"You want to say something?" she asked.

I don't know how she guessed that I had something to tell her. How she had sensed that I was carrying something for her. Girls are great!

"Hmmm... Mr. Ajeeb, you want to say something?" she repeated.

"No....No..... Actually Yes....."

I couldn't switch to the topic I had planned for. I lost confidence. I couldn't make an eye-contact then.

"Okay then, but I thought you were saying something." she said tickling my nerves again.

I found myself helpless. At the backdrop I saw Deepak and Akanksha waving me. They were boosting up my confidence with their hand actions. Deepak joined his hands and begged me, to speak up.

I looked back at her. She was looking at me.

"Actually......... Sonal, I wanted to tell you about a guy who likes you." I said.

"Oh really!" she said sounding surprised.

"Yes Sonal, there is someone who is serious about you." I emphasized.

"Who is the idiot?" she asked.

"He comes in our tuition class, he is in our batch," I used the same strategy.

She smiled.

"His name starts neither with R, nor O," I let her know indirectly that I was talking about myself.

"You talking about yourself Avi?"

I nodded. This caused a weird pause in the conversation. I said nothing, "Avi, you!!" she said, emphasizing the *you*.

I nodded.

"Really….. prove it then." she ordered.

"Proof!!", I was shocked at her weird reaction. She neither accepted my proposal nor refused it. Nobody could make out what was in her mind.

"How should I prove it?" I asked.

"I want to taste the items at each and every stall." she said. "And then I want you to accompany me for a ride on the Giant Wheel".

What a proof she had demanded! Going to each and every stall and tasting the items was mere a thirty minutes job but to accompany her for a ride on the Giant Wheel was rather difficult for me.

I was fond of adventure sports. Speed was my passion. But the rides which follow a circular motion whether horizontally or vertically are something I just can't cope with. My centre of mass gets shifted by the centrifugal action of the circular motion. The radial and the tangential forces get dis-balanced.

I guess I have entered much deeper into the Physics.

Well, we tasted all the junk stuff at the fete and moved towards the Giant Wheel. Sonal knew that I would die but not sit on it. That is why she demanded this as proof.

We reached near the ticket counter. I sweated profusely.

Sitting in the Giant Wheel was like committing suicide. I decided not to go. I literally shivered. I had Giant Wheel phobia!

But even the greatest warriors were bound to bend before women, so where was my stand. I sat with her in the fourth cabin. Slowly, it started moving.

"*Namo Arihantanam, Namo Siddhanam, Namo Aayariyanam, Namo Uvvajhayanam, Namo Loe Savv Sahunam....*" I started praying. Mom has told me that the *mahamantra* helps us to get rid of all the difficulties. I kept on murmuring it continuously.

The wheel started speeding. Sonal was sitting on my left and very excited. I had a tight grip on the supports my right side with my right hand and held Sonal's hand tightly in my left.

"Arpit, do you really like me?" she asked.

How could she be so brutal, I wondered. Asking such a question at such a deadly time was unimaginable. I held my breath as it went faster and faster. It seemed like all my organs were messed up. Heart shifted down to kidneys, lungs moved down to thighs, kidneys to brain, I could feel the movement of junk food inside my stomach.

Sonal was enjoying the thrill of the ride. After seven-eight high speed rounds, I vomitted.

"Yuck!" she said, disgusted.

Her words didn't bother me then. After two-three rounds, the ride stopped.

We stepped out. Deepak helped me clear the stuff. Akanksha brought a Hajmola candy for me to change the bad taste in my mouth.

I took a few minutes to get normal. "What a loser I am!" I said to myself. I was totally disappointed and so was Sonal.

Deepak was pepping me up and Akanksha was talking to her, I don't know about what.

"Sonal, I am not feeling well so I'll be leaving. I just wanted to say you that I like you." I said.

"Avi, let me tell you very frankly." she started.

"I already knew that you were going to propose to me. It was

Akanksha's and my plan to play a prank with you." she giggled. Akanksha joined in the laughter.

I took time to realize that I had been made a fool of. All that happened was pre-planned! They had played with my emotions. I decided not to talk to them forever.

They hurt me and my feelings deeply. I felt an intense pain within. But I managed to remain calm. I was greatly disappointed by Akanksha. Akanksha had been such a true friend of mine; how could she have done that. Whatever had been the reason for such a stupid prank, I decided the it was time to put an end of our relationship.

I went back home without paying any attention to the *masti* they were having. Leaving the fete in a bad mood definitely affected them all but I never cared and went back home, crawled up to my room and slept like dead.

When I woke up, there was no sun in my usually gorgeous-sunny-in-the-morning room and I realized it must be practically mid-day. My first thought was of Sonal. I grabbed my phone and dialled her number, but then I switched it off.

In the evening Akanksha called me up to clear the matter, I didn't talk to her in a friendly way. I requested her to stop disturbing me. I knew I was hurting one of my best pals, but I didn't want to be reminded of the time that was gone. I had prepared myself to forget it all.

I had asked Akanksha to stop calling me and Sonal never dared to. Distances grew between us. One day Akanksha called on my landline and by chance I picked the phone up "Hello, can I talk to Avi, please?" I heard a familiar voice.

"Yes, I am on line" I said.

"Avi, I am sorry for that prank. I beg you to forgive me. Please stop dragging me into it."she said.

I was not able to judge whether the caller was Akanksha or Sonal. "Avi, stop it yaar. It's too much now. I feel sorry about what I did.

Don't you feel that you should forgive me and give your best friend a tight hug?" she said.

I realized that it was Akanksha. She seemed incredibly sweet as she said all this stuff. And I adored her with almost all my heart "Hey Hi......I am sorry too for getting angry with my sweetest friend. But please don't talk about Sonal to me from now on".

"I promise. But please smile"

"Ya….." I said and smiled.

Akanksha kept in touch with me. And gradually I was able to forgive her. We became friends again, as close as we had been earlier. Infact, our friendship grew stronger. But all that Sonal had done had its due effect on me. My feelings for her had out completely died.

Sometimes I felt bad about the gap that had developed between us. But now it was too late for anything to be done. And the day came when we passed out from school. She got through the engineering entrance of Amity University, Noida and I dropped out the year for IIT-JEE preparation.

Jaipur blast in Doon

I didn't clear the IIT-JEE test but secured All India 20324 rank in AIEEE, through which I got a seat of Electronics & Communication Engineering stream at DIT, Dehradun.

"You can teach a student a lesson for a day; but if you can teach him to learn by creating curiosity, he will continue the learning process as long as he lives" is a famous quote by Swami Vivekananda which inspired me a lot.

For every child college life is like a dream, a life which you can enjoy to the fullest, a life which gives you immense opportunities to explore the talent within yourself, and that too when you are in a technical college.

DIT or Dehradun Institute of Technology, Dehradun is a beautiful campus located in the Doon valley which is surrounded by the middle Himalayan ranges at the upper edge and the Shivalik ranges on the lower edge. The waterfall near the campus enhances its beauty fourfold. Bhatta Falls, Shikhar Falls and Robbers Cave are the amazing water beauties surrounding our campus.

Queen of the hills – Mussoorie, is just 15 kms from our college. It's the best freaking out place for guys and gals here. For me it was not very interesting because it was always flooded with the DIT crowd. And I believe that you can't enjoy yourself fully when you are surrounded by people.

9th August 2002, Ragging era DIT, near the Nescafe benches in the campus. Behind the coffee corner, hundreds of students get groomed in the academic block of our institute. The seniors behave like hungry tigers waiting to pounce on us. Every corner of the institute could be seen with a group of seniors firing unpleasant questions and comments on to the new buds.

As darkness fell, a sense of urgency permeated the buildings and the venues adjacent. Inside the college campus the first year students (the freshers) search for places to hide.

For me it was all very normal as I had already made up my mind to face the worse. The *hindi intros, the technical salute, chavvanni-atthani, mussoorie night* were the most common rag-tags of the so called DIT seniors. I really enjoyed them all.

I have always got into naughty situations and the same happened when I cross-ragged one of my batch mate. The scene took place late at night in the apartment number 305 of boys hostel block III. The boys hostel block III is limited for the accommodation of fresh intakes of the students by the institute in the bachelor of technology and management courses. The block was a four storeyed building and had 64 studio apartments. Each apartment had 3 two-seater rooms and a common living room. I had my accommodation in apartment number 408. It was the place where I visualized the ground realities of student life.

My one year stay in hostel made me go through the grass root realities of youth. Smoking, taking drugs, boozing and getting laid with girls were quite common among the students residing in the hostels. To me it was all very new but never excited me. My ethics, my culture, my tradition and my upbringing stood firmly right in front of me all the time, to protect me and even prevent me from getting into the wrong direction.

The academic session started on 1st August 2002.

I remember the attire forced on us by our seniors to be carried to the college. Black pleated trousers with white or yellow shirt tightly tucked in, sports shoes without socks and no wrist watches and belts was the dress code to be followed by all the newcomers in the college.

Neha, let me try explaining my college life via this short poem, I hope you like it. It was written by one of my close friends.

It was just another Monday morning
As I stepped through my college gates wondering
What did today have in store for me?
May be a reason to put this in my date in my diary?

I greeted the college gaurds as they
Tried to stop students on bikes zooming away
The poor gaurd just mumbled and grumbled
And swore to deflate the tyres to get even!

Students poured out from the bus and looked totally haggled
Like they just won a battle they don't want to remember!
Everyone walked on bye, I spared a moment
To marvel at the scenery that envelopes my college

Mountains encircle this modern structure
And a stream runs in the valley on the side
The sun comes from somewhere behind these hills
It's like a beautiful picture come to life!

Checking their reflection in the rearview mirror
Guys quicken their ties and fix their hair
Girls giggled in groups and gossip a fair share
And hustled up the winding stairs

I never reached the lecture hall well in time
And had chose a seat that served as a vantage point
I sat back and spread my notes on the desk
And got busy copying the tutorial from a friend!

The hooter, which is such a terrible siren
Went off as the professor started the lecture
Of course not all will be smooth
For the first lecture is reserved for late come-ers!

The poor professor tries to reprimand them for being late
We enjoy as more time gets wasted
The late comer, who is not even out of breath
Humors the class with excuses so lame!

In the lecture right before lunch break
Anticipation and boredom is etched on every face
Yawns are stifled, the watch seems stuck
And plans for lunch are made on sms's

People scramble out of the lecture halls
A new glee is experienced as the cafeteria beckons
But a coke bottle smashed, and a fight broke out
But all was settled as the Dean appeared on the spot

After we fought a raging battle
For some chairs and a table and sardarji's attention
Me and my friends settled with our lunch
And the variety of youngsters grabbed my attention

There are some who always have
A book the size of a brick in their hands
And then there are those who dont even know
What subjects they have to study that sem!

There are some who wear the latest fashions
And there are those who'd know every gossip and rumour
There are some who are friends with the whole college
And there are some who know no-one but their girlfriend!

Diverse though they are, there is so much in common
And as I look beyond I see
The abstract that engulfs the entire college

I see hope and fear and joys and tears
I see animated discussions and laughter and chatter
The vibrance and color fills aspirations
I see love being spilt and dreams being spun

I made my way back to the hostel
Past the humming computer lab I walked
Right above the electronics lab buzzed
The mechanical lab clattered on

I checked my day for signs of excitement
Will today go down in my diary tonight?
hmm..no nothing extraordinary took place
It was just another college day....

I was happy with myself, I used to enjoy in my own world when one day........I dared to bunk the lecture one of the deadliest lecturer of the institute. I just don't remember how it slipped from my mind that nothing goes as per my planning and it has to get worse for me.

The same happened.

The teacher saw me when I was jumping out from the rear window.

'Who was that? Stop him!' shouted he to the class.

I guess that sometimes destiny plays a significant role. As I was successful in running away from the scene. I was running as fast as I could to hide myself. A tremendous energy was felt within which was helping me in heading towards the hostel at much greater speed.

As soon as I took a turn from the Nescafe kiosk towards the hostel gate, a girl appeared right in front. My reflexes gave up and indicated that now it was not possible to cross her safely. I had no option left!

Both of us fell on the ground. I got bruised.

I was lying over her trying to untangle myself. I was helpless.

Some of her friends helped us.

The girl was very simple and had a natural beauty. She had a unique attraction. She was wearing a sea green salwar suit with matching bindi and large ear-rings. She had an ideal cuteness which was highlighted by her innocent expression of feeling sorry about the accident. For few next seconds I felt as if I had a nervous breakdown, I kept staring at her. She had long black hair cut in steps which she left open, a curl carelessly on her forehead. Her hair was so silky that it reflected light and a beautiful sight of seven colors could be easily identified. Her face had a natural cute shape; a small pink nose, rudely cheeks, sincere eyes and lovely lips.

I felt as if I had seen her somewhere; somehow she must be related to me. Was it a divine coincidence? Or it was just my perception? I just kept looking at her.

"I am sorry" she uttered very softly as if she was talking to herself.

I was totally lost in her so didn't bother to notice her innocent request. While she was managing to arrange her *dupatta*, I picked her books and gently handled them to her. She smiled and went off.

'Avinash', 'Avinash', I heard someone shouting. I turned around and saw my Chemistry professor approaching me with a frowning expression.

I was still unconscious.

Was it love at first sight? Or was it an infatuation? Or simply a crush....?? Why did I feel as if I had seen her somewhere?

"What are you doing here? I will report you to the Dean this", the professor shouted at me.

I stood silent. I was punished!!

Love at first sight

From gardens to waterfalls, beaches to movie halls, gol-gappa shops to shopping malls I kept going on outings with her in my own imagination until I realized that someone or the other faculty member was shouting at me. Day and night I kept dreaming about her. I used to think about romantic scenes, I used to replace the starring of romantic Hollywood movies with me and her. God…I was lost!!

She didn't appear for the whole of next week.

I started my search for her because she was not just my imagination. It became my habit to miss alternate lectures and sit in café, I used to stand near notice boards, I visited the library twice a day, I killed time at STD shop……and at all the places where maximum density of students was observed. I experienced some of the most beautiful days of my life; everything seemed to be so beautiful – so lovely. Five days passed away, I didn't find her.

My search ended when one day a group of two boys and two girls entered our lecture hall to make some announcements. It was like a dream come true to see her again that too in my own classroom, standing right in front of me and delivering kind a speech. "So who can perform it right now?" one of them said. I was constantly staring at her which turned into a long eye-contact. I guess she recognized that event. I raised my hand just to show confidence. I heard a pompous laughter of the class. I regained my senses and soon discovered that I had made a fool of myself. They were enquiring for somebody to dance like a eunuch for a stage play to be performed for the cultural event to be held soon in the college. I had no choice but to perform in front of my classmates. The embarrassment which I was feeling turned into big smiles when she laughed madly seeing my performance. The class was laughing too, but frankly speaking- I didn't bother to notice. I was then asked to give in my personal details for their database for the same function, *I was selected for the role.*

'Thank you ma'am', I was supposed to say but didn't!! I was literally not in my senses.

The song,

> *Ek ladki ko dekha to aisa laga*
> *Ek Ladki ko dekha to aisa laga,*
> *Jaise khilta gulab*
> *Jaise shayar ka khwab*
> *Jaise ujli kiran*
> *Jaise van mein hiran*
> *Jaise mandir mein ho ek jalta diyaaaaaaa.......*

was getting recalled.

'What a wonderful performance! You must try for the Boogie-Woogie', said Ria. I was trying to hide myself.

'You dance so well, you can entertain people! You were lovely dude', laughed Ria.

I could have committed suicide for that. But the lovely smile of Cheeku was taking me far away from the real world. Cheeku was the name - my imagination gave to her. Yes I was completely lost. Before this I used to think that it all happens in movies.

'Avi, are you listening to me? I was complimenting you, so please stop feeling bad! We all really liked it', emphasized Ria.

You must be wondering of who Ria is? Well, she is someone on whom I can write a book. But let me tell you briefly about her.

She has a sweet smile with a lovely style
She has beautiful eyes but when she cries
She has a sparkling face, an outstanding knowledge-base
She is smart and cute, She is caring and rarely mute
She always pulls my leg and forces me to beg
She can never see me cry, I can't really even try
She is always there for me, how high may the tides be
She is Ria, my friend!

I think that would be sufficient to portray an outline of her in your mind. Well, my friend circle came to know about my crush for Cheeku.

Many questions kept on running in my mind about her. Was it simply a crush? Or was it a true love?

I had been in touch with so many girls right from my school life, but I had never felt before the acute interest, I felt in her. I liked the way she smiled, I liked the way she apologized at our first meeting, I liked the way she carried her books, I liked the way she made announcements for the cultural show, I simply liked the way she was.

That day when she went out after selecting me for the role of eunuch, I wanted to move out of the lecture hall and take another look at her. But that could not be done. I felt that scores of students sitting inside the class were all watching me.

Why was I thinking about her so much? Was it her looks? Was it because the beautiful smile she carried? Had I met her before? Why did she seem to be known? I was puzzled, greatly puzzled.

That evening I went back to hostel very preoccupied. I couldn't control my feeling for her. I was dying to see her again. But I didn't know who she was? Which stream and semester she belonged too? Yes, she was definitely my senior as only seniors are allowed to make announcements in the classes.

Next day I sat in the cafeteria for over an hour. She didn't come. Several groups of students came and sprawled all over the place, but not she. I walked along the pathway from the cafeteria's entrance to the cash-counter a number of times, peering furtively at every group. It was a very keen search, but it brought forth nothing. Why wasn't she anywhere? My heart beat faster at the sight of every figure that approached in salwar-suit.

I saw her in the library next day. She was wearing a black salwar-suit and pondering upon some science journals. I saw her from a distance and went towards her as if drawn by a rope. But on approaching her, my courage failed me, and I diverted my direction.

It is so difficult to approach someone whom you actually want a relationship with.

I stopped and blamed myself for wasting a good opportunity of making my person familiar to her, I turned once again with the intention of passing before her closely and wishing her if get noticed. At a distance I could look at her, I could see the prettiest woman of the world just ten yards away from me. I really mean it when I call her the prettiest woman of the world.

I walked towards her hiding my eyes from everyone else in the library. When I came close I felt self-conscious and awkward and while passing actually in front of her, I bent my head, fixed my gaze on the other book-shelves and walked fast. I was away, many shelves away from her in a moment.

I hoped that she had observed me. I stood there and debated with myself whether she had seen me or not.

She hadn't. She was busy flipping the pages of the journals.

I was standing near the shelves of Mechanical section, which must have been around fifteen meters away from the racks where journals were kept. Some of my friend once told me that *staring is half the victory in love*. So, I found a place in front of hers though three tables apart and kept my eyes on her.

But that day even I couldn't get her to talk.

The next day, I saw her in the audience of the basketball match. She was sitting with her friends and cheering for the team in blue. The intra-college basketball tournament was on and that day was a match between Electronics & Communication and Industrial Production teams. The players of Industrial Production team were in blue and of my stream were in green.

I was least bothered about the match. The only thing I liked about the match was that I could find her stream. She was cheering for the guys in blue so definitely she was from Industrial Production stream. I had determined to stare at her continuously in the evening. I worked according to the magic formula of *Staring*. I was actually collecting a lot of details regarding her extra-ordinary features.

She had a lovely figure, a slight and slender one, beautifully fashioned, sparkling eyes fair complexion. When she drank something, it could be seen going down her throat, she had such a delicate appearance. Forgive me Neha, if you are find me sounding poetic, but I am telling you what I felt. I sat at some distance and kept throwing her a side glance every tenth second. I noticed that she played a great deal with her friends, watching the match. I couldn't stop looking at her.

This optical communion became a daily habit. My powers of observation and deduction increased tremendously. I gathered several facts about the girl. She loved wearing dark colors. Dark colors suited her fair complexion. She came to the library every alternate day. She came late to the college on Wednesdays and Saturdays. Maybe because we are allowed to wear casuals on both these days and don't mind but girls take hell lot of time in getting ready, choosing the best outfits and wearing the make-up.

I lived over a month in a state of bliss. I began to feel that I ought to be up and be a little more practical. I could not just go on staring at her all my life.

I was not able to find a solution to my problem. I called up my sweetest friend and guide at home – my Bhabhi, and told her the complete story, right from day one. Bhabhi understands me well and is a very good guide in such matters. After listening to my story she could sense the intense love in my feelings for her. She suggested to me to approach her first and ask her to be my friend. I tried to talk to her daily but couldn't. I didn't know what happened to me whenever I tried to approach her. I would always lose my strength. My condition became pathetic. One day Ria said "Avi, shame on you. It's been months and you are not able to talk to her. Now either you talk to her today itself or forget her for ever." Her words shook my heart. I decided to talk to her and propose friendship.

And the day came. I had gone to ISBT to drop one of my friends. I saw her there. I will never forget meeting her at the bus stand by chance. I was not sure why she was there. I couldn't see any of her friends with her. But then I noticed a big bag in her hand. I figured that she was going home. The first thought in my mind was to board the same bus she could take. It is difficult to describe my condition fully. On one hand there were my internal exams, sessionals we call them here and on other hand my love. I cannot say which of the two moved me more at that instant but on second thought I did not mind missing my exams. I parked my bike at the ISBT parking, withdrew cash from the ATM, bought a ticket for the same bus she was going.

How I suddenly managed to muster up courage I do not know. Nothing daunted me, and without the slightest hesitation I boarded the bus. The situation turned dramatic as I didn't carry any luggage.

Not even a small hand bag and I had the helmet with me. No one can explain the attraction between the two human beings. It happens.

She was sitting in the third row, probably her seat number was nine. My seat number was twenty nine. I requested the gentleman sitting on seat number thirteen to exchange his seat with mine. After a long session of convincing him the reason, I won. I was seated just behind her. I felt anxiety, joy, fear and great happiness – everything at the same time. I wondered "What if she doesn't recognize me?" I was countering my own thoughts.

She plugged in the ear phones of i-pod and lay back on her seat. She moved her seat back to the fullest. Her face was now clearly visible to me. I was feeling like kissing her lips passionately. But how was that to be done? All kinds of impossible thoughts kept crossing my mind. I began building castles in the air. Thirty minutes passed and I could do nothing. I then asked the conductor for mineral water, though I was not feeling thirsty. I did it just to show my presence. But it didn't bother her. *"Bhayia kitne baje pahochenge Dilli?"* I asked the conductor just to get noticed. It didn't work either. Bloody i-pod became the hurdle between me and my love. I couldn't fight the feeling any longer. I stood up and went to the Driver's cabin, pretending to check the AC temperature. I was nervous to see her face make eye contact. But when I was returning, I could make an eye-contact with her. Surprisingly she smiled. "Hi" she exclaimed.

My heartbeat zoomed to about a thousand beats per minute and I couldn't help smiling back. "Hi! My name is Avinash", I said.

She scrutinized me thoroughly. "Of course, I know you". I smiled affably, my best smile, as if I had been asked for it by a photographer.

"Ma'am, you going to Delhi too?" I don't know why I asked this stupid question.

"Ya, its my hometown." she said.

"Oh that's great. That is wonderful." I said. I didn't know why I was being so stupid.

"Where are you going by the way? You have exams in college na?"

"I am debarred." I said proudly. Getting debarred in the college was like a trend. More than fifty percent of the total students in our class remained debarred in the internal examinations. Actually it indicated that the student was not the book-worm types.

"That's bad." she said in a dull voice. "So, are your friends with you?" she asked.

"No, not in this bus." I said.

"Why don't you come here then?" She pointed the seat next to hers.

Without a moment's pause I nodded "Ya sure, it would be my pleasure."

I couldn't believe what was happening with me. Accidental meeting her at the bus stop, boarding the same bus, sitting near my love all seemed like a film on. I shifted to the seat next to hers. Seat number ten. Ten became my lucky number from then onwards.

I waited for her to say something. But she was too polite to open a conversation. I asked "You remember me ma'am?"

"How can one forget your extraordinary dance dear?" she replied with a joyous laugh.

I felt a bit embarrassed about the way I had to perform in the class. But my mind went blank because of her presence. "I even remember the day when you collided with me, hurting my knee." she added. Wow! She remembered our first meeting. That was enough for me to spend my whole life.

"Tell me about yourself." she demanded.

"What can I say?" I confessed, touched by her interest and not wishing to let it go unrewarded. I hesitated, wondered how to start. This was my first independent conversation the divine creature. I might make a fool of myself or win the heavens. How should I announce myself? I gathered up courage and started introducing myself. Thank god I did it in a very impressive manner. I disclosed all my notorious interests and activities first. It made her laugh. Then I told her about my hobbies, interests, place I belonged to, family, career plans etcetra etcetra. I got all the information from her side also. We were becoming friends.

"I am in Industrial Production second year" she said.

I had a sudden, perfect flash into the future. *Director, Jain Industries* was the designation I assigned to her at that very moment, but in my own dreams. "Wow, so you would be fit into large-scale industries then", I said appreciating her decision for choosing the Industrial Production branch. Actually I would have appreciated her for any *xyz* branch she would have chosen. I was so lost in her.

"26ᵗʰ March" I said.

"What?" she said. She appeared puzzled.

"That's my date of birth. What about yours?" I asked.

"*Kyu? Gift khareedna hai kya?*" she giggled.

I love this sweet attitude of girls. I loved the way she giggled at this. "Yes, the gift needs to be rare and precious for a rare and precious beauty." I said with full confidence, looking straight into her eyes.

"You're a flirt Avi." she said, pulling my cheeks.

It was the tiniest physical contact, but it made my heart zoom. I smiled.

She called me a flirt and was still talking to me! That made it clear that she was not taking me to be the wrong type. I continued. I touched her shawl, "What are you wearing by the way. You look so pretty! This color is a touch of genius."

She opened her eyes wide "Really."

"Sure," I said.

I was crazy enough about her to tell her whatever she wanted to hear. The trouble was I didn't know what she wanted to hear. I didn't know how to continue with my soft-skills of flattering her. We then, started with our likes and dislikes. Topics untouched, topics of no relevance were being discussed and enjoyed by both of us. We were finding each other's company good. She disclosed her turn ons and offs. She even showed me her favorite list of songs in her I-pod. She felt like talking her mind to me.

I found a new person in her. The first day I saw her, I thought she was a shy girl who was not open and friendly. But she was so friendly, it completely changed my first impression of her. But yes she was as sweet and as decent as I had figured out on day one.

Even before reaching the midway of Dehradun-Delhi route, I had shared all my secrets with her. I was finding it a great pleasure. I even found that she was taking interest in knowing more and more about me. She put her fist on mine and said "It is a miracle to find a friend like you Avi. I have never been so talkative. I have never told anyone many of the things I shared with you I don't know why I am feeling like talking to you till the endless time".

I was deeply touched by her words and her second touch made my head reel for a moment. I couldn't see anything clearly. Everything disappeared into a sweet, dark haze, as if I was under chloroform. Was this the right time to tell her that I loved her? Or should I wait for some divine moment? I was confused. A number of courageous thoughts were coming to in my mind. If they succeeded it would lead to a triumphant end, if it failed I didn't know what would happen.

"Ma'am, I even shared with you the secrets which I have never told anybody earlier." I said. And I held her hand a bit tightly. She smiled, with her eyes a little wet. Analyzing the sentiments I then told her straightaway that her smile was beautiful. Anyone likes to hear flattering comments, especially girls. I praised her beauty whenever I could snatch a moment. I was making some impression on her now.

Wild ideas started cropping up in my mind. I thought of kissing her, I thought of smooching her. I thought of making love to her. Huh..! I shook my head to clear it. "Avi, you are a real flirt, I can say" she said, pinching the skin above my elbow. "Flirt!!! I was telling the truth" I said. "You are.......... You have a naughty brain" she said. We laughed together.

After about four hours the bus stopped at Cheetal Grand, a resort halfway through the journey. The bus driver informed all the passengers to be back in fifteen minutes. We remained seated in the bus. It was cold outside and we were not willing to freeze. "What'll you have?" I asked. "Anything vegetarian" she replied, not wanting to be difficult. I regarded her thoughtfully. "Are you a vegetarian?" I asked. "Won't you talk to me if I eat non-veg?" she questioned in a taunting tone. Before I could understand the notion she said "Well, being a Jain I can't just think of eating non-veg." Her words thrilled me greatly as even I am a Jain. I started daydreaming about our marriage. I could imagine her in bridal getup. I could see Mom and Dad giving us their blessings. I could see myself dressed in *Sherwani*. My heart was full of with undying excitement.

I was looking anxiously at her, I was expecting her to reveal some more facts about herself. "What happened? Go get something to eat." she shook my hand.

I was still in my thoughts.

"I know it is cold outside but sweetie I am feeling hungry." she said soothingly. Her words were enough to arouse me. She has called me her sweetie! I had heard from my friends that girls call boys sweetie, honey, cheeku-pie, hubby-dubby when they are in love with them. So had I won the battle of winning her heart? I didn't know. What I knew was that I was ready to do anything for her at that moment. Her sweetness made me crazy. I kissed her cheek and jumped out of the bus to get some vegetarian stuff to eat. I didn't bother to think about the way she was going to react. I didn't bother to notice the people around. It just happened all of a sudden and spontaneously.

I got back some patties and french-fries. She was trying to wrap herself in the quilt. I felt as if she was in my bedroom. Sorry let me correct myself, in our bedroom, I had already considered her mine and was ready to share everything with her, and I was serving her meals on the bed. I sat beside her and offered her the *veg* stuff. Suddenly the word *veg* gained importance in my life. She was still arranging the quilt, covering herself to restrict the entry of even a tiny whiff of add air.

"I am sorry....... I ....I kissed you" I bowed my head before her. She didn't utter a word. I remained in the same position, requesting her forgiveness. She kissed me on the head and said, "You are dear to me Avi. You are my friend". My soul danced with joy. I felt as if I had won the world. My heart was in the seventh heaven. I was experiencing the most memorable moment of my life. "Now stop talking and eat it first. You must be hungry" I said, planting a smacking kiss on her cheek. She gave me a sweet and an inviting look. "Sorry for that...........please have them" I said.

She leaned on my shoulder after finishing the patties. I was slowly putting the french-fries into her mouth. After finishing them through she said she wanted a short nap. I patted her, stored her cheeks and ears and hair. Slowly she felt asleep. I kissed her forehead and lay my temporal on hers. It is really difficult to explain what I felt at that moment. That feeling can only be felt when you actually get into a serious relationship. We realized that Delhi had arrived only when the conductor switched on the lights. The bus stopped at ISBT Kashmiri Gate. It showed four sharp in the clock. It was time to say goodbye but I didn't get up from the seat. I did not want her to leave. I was missing the absence of the time-machine in the world.

"Won't you come to see-me off?" she asked, for which I was not at all ready. I could not see my love go. We got down from the bus as her father had come to receive her. "Pa, this is Avi" she introduced me to her father. "*Namaste Uncle*" I bowed with hands joined. "Thanks *beta* for accompanying Lisha till here" he said to me. "Please don't thank me Sir. Infact, she accompanied me." I said and smiled to Lisha. They then waved me off. "Bye Avi" she said. I didn't respond and stood still.

Lisha looked back, hiding from her father, she passed me a flying kiss. Neha, you can imagine what the state of my mind could have been.

I boarded the very next bus to Jaipur. Three hours passed and still I was sitting in the same position though on different seats. I was obsessed with thoughts of her. I reveled in memories of the hours I had spent with her. The kisses we had shared were getting recalled. I leaned back a little on my seat and opened my eyes wide. I could not remember a more miserable period of my life. The usual symptoms were present, of course: no taste for food, no sound sleep, no stability, I couldn't stay put on one seat, no peace of mind – no, no, no, a number of no's. I was sitting on my chair, elbow on the arm support, chin on my fist. I had never felt so vacant before. I was not able to rest.

I shifted about in my seat, tucked my jacket in tightly and thought of the days ahead, lying back in the darkness and just letting my mind wander, I messaged her "Hi…. Missing your company"

My mobile beeped after a few minutes and it was a reply from Lisha "m missin u 2. Tk Cr. C ya soon."

The messages then kept pouring in and out. Neither of us was bothered about our phone balances being screwed. The roaming charges for her and the pre-paid non free SMS pack for me. "Avi, I am not able to sleep. Thinking of you", her message said. I revealed that I had escaped my internal exams just to spend time with her. She was shocked and surprised. "dat ws so unfair on ur part Avi. u wl hv 2 suffr in internl assessmnt" she messaged back. "Why did you do that Avi?" she asked in her next SMS.

"Because my life is so blank without your presence" I replied back.

For the next thirty minutes she didn't reply. She must have taken it the other way. My courage, my love, my feelings for her were getting drowned. Had I committed a blunder? I messaged again "I am sorry Lisha but I can't steal stop thinking of you. I like you."

She didn't reply.

I reached Jaipur but my cell phone didn't beep. I was anxiously looking at its screen, wanting it to beep. But it didn't. I reached home and straightaway went to my room. Everybody at home thought I was tired after such a long journey, so didn't disturbed me at all. I lay down on my bed and looked out of the window. I saw the construction going on in the new multi-storey projects in our lane. The sky was crystal-clear, it must have been nine in morning. Having a lot of questions in my mind, I started drawing my own conclusions. I started recalling her face and the talks we had, looking out at the sky.

I started painting her portrait in the milk-white clouds. I stretched myself on the bed and fell asleep don't know when. The noon sun shone directly on my face. I sat up rubbing my eyes. I checked out my cell phone. I found thirteen missed calls and four messages. All of them were from Lisha. I quickly scanned all of them to find out if everything was okay.

YES it was.

The communication gap between us had been bridged now. She battled against herself whether to ask me or not. But by the time she decided to, her fingers had already reacted faster than her mind. The message was sent. "Avi I lovd ur company. Infact I…….. yes I do".

I exclaimed in joy, jumped here and there in the room and the dining hall. I kissed Bhabhi and Mummy. I had gone crazy for obviously some reason. Some very big reason. I started dancing like Amir Khan in the some *Pehla Nasha* with Bhabhi, imagining her to be Lisha. She was surprised.

"What is the matter bhayia?" she asked me giggling. "*Kyun chalti hai pawan, kyu jhoome hai gagan, kyu machalta hai mann…….na aap jano na hum*" I sang and answered.

"*Koi ladki ka chakkar hai kya? Main teri taange tod doongi*" Mom intervened. "Nai Maa, nothing like that. I am happy to pay a surprise visit. That's all." I said.

"*Koi pyar-vyar ka chakkar mat chalana*" Mom instructed. Bhabhi started laughing at me. She loved to pull my leg. "*Maa, Bhagwan Mahaveer ne kaha hai ki is shrishti mei sabse pyar karo*" I dared to tickle her Hitler bone. She was left with no answer as she is a great devotee of

Lord Mahaveer. And whenever I surprise her she has only one thing to say *Papa ko aane de, sab batati hu. Fir karna sabse pyar.* And we all laughed together.

"For how many days have you made your program Avi?" Mom asked. "I had already missed college for three consecutive days without any leave application, so I need to go back as early as possible." I said.

"That's not fair. You have come a long way. Plan three day stay" Mom insisted. "I will see to it." I said and hugged her.

That day the evening passed at home. All were busy pulling my leg on a number of points. Mom was busy inquiring about my girlfriends, if any, Bhabhi was helping Mom in delving deeper into the question, Bhayia was asking about my heavy expenses and Tinni was busy reading the messages in my inbox loudly. Thanks to the thought which had made me clear all the messages when I had woken up in noon.

The whole night we kept on messaging to each other. All of them were reflecting on the intensity at which we were missing each other. Some of our messages had no relevance at all. We enjoyed disturbing each other every fifteen minutes till the next evening when I called her. I was calling her to ask her plan of returning back to Dehradun. My heart was beating hard with excitement about speaking to her for the first time on phone. The phone rang for a long time. If it hadn't been a bonafide emergency, I'd have surely hung up. But I waited, pacing the floor in my baggy pajamas and finally, she picked up.

"Hi", I said awkwardly.

"Hi" she whispered. "How are you?"

"I am fine. I was missing you" I dared to say.

"Same here Avi" she said, a bit nervous.

I stood speechless. An awkward pause followed. I desperately wanted to keep her on the phone but couldn't think of anything to say. I was feeling conscious, don't know why.

She broke the silence and said "So wassup?"

"Nothing much. I am leaving for Doon tomorrow. When are you planning to go?"

"I was planning for day after" she replied.

"Oh......" I was trying to emerge from the shock.

"Why don't you postpone your plan for a day?" she requested, but it sounded as if she was ordering me.

"Done." I said.

"Good then meet you the day after, Bye Avi" she said and hung off.

I changed my plan of leaving for Dehradun the next day.

"Mom, I will be leaving day after tomorrow." I shouted, not caring where Mom was and whether she had heard me or not.

In the evening...................

Rang De Basanti "Treat"

"**W**ant to eat anything," mom voiced her most frequently quoted line from the kitchen.

"No, Mom I am going out with Nischay. We will be going out for Dinner," I replied.

"Tomorrow you are leaving. Don't you have any time for us?"

"Mummy I am not leaving tomorrow. I have postponed it by a day," I said.

"Postpone….."

"Please don't ask me the reason now." I said and hugged her.

"*Avi Bhayia* there is someone at the door asking for you," said my sis Tinni.

"Who's that?" I enquired.

'I didn't ask the name. May be he is one of your tuition friends." replied Tinni.

'Hey Arjun! How are you? Long time no see........', louded me in an excited voice.

Arjun has been my junior in Mahaveer Public School, where I did my Senior Secondary from. Arjun is a smart chap who has always been good at sports. Basketball, Cricket were the ones in which he used to perform superbly.

"Bhayia, you are looking great in this short hair-cut." he said.

"Thank you very much for the compliment dude. I am going to Nischay's place for dinner. Why don't you join us?" I asked.

Arjun was not willing.

"Some other day. You guys carry on," he requested.

"Oh cum'on, don't behave like a shy chick. We will have loads of fun. Come lets go." I urged him.

"But I have to be back home by 12. Otherwise I'll be thrown out of the house!" Arjun said.

"Don't worry dude." I assured.

We then drove to Nischay's place.

Nischay greeted us warmly.

We made our den in his guest room. All three of us were recalling the fun we had during our school days. Missing lectures, bunking assembly, punishments, home work, games period, the school building, the pathetic staff, colleagues and of course the hot-chicks were all discussed.

After killing about an hour, boredom started dominating our mind and we were feeling sleepy. To cut the crap I suggested something new, something adventurous. Arjun got a bit scared to hear the idea of trying adventure at this point of hour.

"Why don't we go to the *Rang de Basanti* place? And we will recollect our sweet memories in the beauty of nature." I suggested.

Rang de Basanti place is a *Baawri*, a huge water reservoir of ancient times, at the topmost corner of the Nahargarh Fort. Nahargarh fort is amongst the wonderful architectural marvels of Jaipur city. The city has a number of royal forts and palaces depicting the glorious past of the land of Rajasthan.

"I hope you are not out of your head Avi!", shouted Nischay. "Just look at the time dude! It is very late now. Let us plan for tomorrow morning!" said he in a convincing tone.

"Dudes, it would be great fun. We would take some other route to maintain our excitement of reaching the top." said I looking straight into their eyes.

"I am going back home!" said Arjun and he stood up. Nischay agreed to my idea, as he normally did to whatever I had to say about adventure.

Adventure had been an essential part of my life. Wherever I went I made it a point to discover the newest routes. I had been fortunate in that my curiosity had taken me to very beautiful but deadly places that opened up my mind to the cosmic reality.

"We can do something else to kill time" said Nischay.

"Nischay we must not kill time, rather use it to enjoy to the fullest. Please give a second thought to my idea," I said.

"My idea works for all of us. And we don't have any other choice than to go bed, do we?"

Nischay was convinced for the fun. Arjun was pissed with us anyway.

It was Tuesday. The thirteen kilometer stretch leading from Nischay's house in Shastri Nagar to the freak out place Nahargarh fort normally took thirty minutes to cover. But the new machines which we were riding made us reach in less than twenty minutes.

All three of us were thrilled to rock the Nahargarh fort at midnight. It was pitch dark outside. I could hardly see anyone beyond the three of us. On the highway we came across some heavily loaded trucks and some policemen patrolling.

I found that Nischay and I preferred freaking out late at night. I mean we enjoyed the anonymity it gave us. Because during the day wherever you go, whatever you do, people look twice. So, you can not be original in your actions. And in my opinion if your originality suffers, your existence suffers.

And Neha that's why today I feel as if I am not living, those are the gone days.

Well, let me not get into all that philosophy. We started off from Nischay's place at around 2:30. Nischay and I were on Karizma and Arjun was on my Activa.

When we reached at the down-hills of the Nahargarh Fort, we took a break at the road side dhaba. These road side dhabas in the plain areas are open 24 x 7. They really serve delicious meals. Without wasting much of our time we bought coke cans and wafers and then left for our final destination which was now just 4 kms uphill.

The sight of the road was frightening. It was covered on both sides by dry trees and a dense undergrowth. Some of the trees seemed like ghosts hanging in the air with their arms spread out. It felt as if they were inviting us to the castle of horror. There was an eerie silences everywhere The only thing which could only be heard was the sound of insects.

"Avi, don't you feel that we must return" asked Nischay.

"Are you afraid of ghosts?" I laughed.

"Bhayia it's too dark here. I suggest we leave. We can come back in the morning." said Arjun.

"I have heard that there are some wild animals in these hills." Nischay added.

I kept on countering each of their excuses. I was very talkative and I found it easy. Actually when you talk more about ideas and logic it so happens that some constructive idea or the other strikes your medulla oblongata.

"Medualla Oblongata? Were you a biology student? " Neha asked.

I had never been a biology student Neha, but medulla oblongata is the control house of the brain.

Now apart from the sound the insects were making, I could be heard. We were heading upwards.

As soon as we reached the final stretch of the road at the top, we found a bike following us. I don't know where it came from but it appeared all of a sudden.

"Stop right here!" shouted the person on the pillion.

For the first instance all three of us thought them to be the patrolling cops. But they were not in uniform first. Second, they didn't look like cops, I mean the number plate of the bike didn't have the sign 'Police', there was no *laathi* in their hand.

Nischay was slowing down.

"Just stop I said you fuckers." the rider shouted.

I sensed something fishy.

"Nischay they are not the cops. Don't stop." I alarmed though I was frightened.

They crossed Arjun, who was on Activa and came very near us, hardly a meter away. I saw the pillion rider taking out a knife. The knife glittered due to the reflection of Activa's head-light.

My heart froze. It seemed as if my blood had stopped flowing.

"Run Nischay! They are carrying a knife."

Nischay felt the sensitivity of the situation sensing terror in my voice. He went faster.

"Stop or else we will hurt you fuckers." they shouted.

I suggested Nischay to keep on driving fast and just be conscious while taking the turns. One wrong turn and we could have slid down hundreds of meters.

"Why the hell you are not accelerating?" shouted I at Nischay.

"Avi, what about Arjun? They will catch hold on him" Nischay replied.

Our condition became worse. I kept my eye on Arjun.

"Arjun keep on driving faster." I kept louding.

But then I saw something that amazed me. I was astonished to see that they were not following all three of us. But they made me and Nischay their targets. Arjun was left behind and they started chasing us.

"Run back Arjun." I shouted.

But he kept on following us.

"Drive back idiot and get some help." I shouted again.

But the idiot fellow kept on following. I don't know what was going in his mind.

"Nischay, those guys are following us not Arjun. Arjun is behind them. You drive fast now." I said.

Nischay speeded like hell. I would like to thank the developing team at Hero Honda which produced such an amazing machine. We gave a good lead to the bastards but soon later, the next fear conquered our mind and that was the dead end ahead.

Several thoughts of retaliating came to our mind but the optimal one was, we were confused to make a quick decision. We planned to hide ourselves and Karizma in the bushes.

Quickly we hid the bike behind a tree. We rushed to hide ourselves in the bushes. I picked a big stone. I guess that was giving me confidence in tackling the situation. The guys on blue TVS Victor were heading forward in search for us.

Nischay suddenly rushed towards their bike with a brick in his hand and then without giving even a seconds pause, smashed their headlight. Perhaps he did so as to disable their visibility. Whatever it was, but it was increasing my confidence as now they would not be able to chase us again.

I threw a stone targeting the pillion rider's head. '*Bloody bastards! You want to play game with us! Take this...*' shouted I at the top of my voice. I grabbed the pillion rider's collar and gave eight non-stop slaps across his face. By that time Nischay smashed the fuel tank. He grabbed the head of the guy driving the bike and smashed it into the handle. Blood spurted out of his nose.

Arjun was shocked to see all this. He shivered in fear.

I held the pillion guy in an elbow lock. He was struggling to breathe.

'Leave him', pleaded Arjun. I gripped him tighter. 'Please cut the crap bhayia!', he requested again.

'Whats going on here?', Arjun cried.

I kicked the boys face and released him. Both the guys kneeled on the floor and sucked in air. The last kick on his face smeared the blood from his nose across his face.

'Avi, now run! It is not safe to be here', said Nischay. He started the bike.

'We need to reach the main road as early as possible', Nischay suggested. 'Cumm'on Arjun lets go. Follow us!' shouted I and jumped on Karizma. Arjun didn't respond as if he had a nervous breakdown.

'Arjun, what the hell are you doing? Turn the Activa and run!' shouted I in a raucous pitch. But he stood dumb.

The guys were still lying on the road.

'It would be definitely better for us to clear the scene as soon as possible', said me to myself. But I realized that for Arjun it was not possible to drive, he was frightened. By that time the guys managed to start their bike. I could see the anger in their actions. I quickly sat off Karizma and ran towards Arjun.

'Avi are you mad…. The guys are definitely going to follow us. Come back' shouted Nischay.

But I headed towards Arjun in a heroic style, though it was really risky for me, to do that without any backup plan. Sometimes it automatically happens when an intense energy is felt within, how I don't know.

"Avi make it fast! They are coming!" shouted Nischay.

I pulled Arjun apart from the Activa and made him sit with Nischay on Karizma. I ran back to Activa.

The guys on the bike were hardly ten meters away from me when I started the Activa. They were carrying the knife I knew.

Nothing was in my mind but to run.

We started speeding downhill at the maximum of our engine capacities. When you believe your mind finds ways to do. We kept on switching off our headlights to create the disability of vision for the guys following us. It was very dangerous, as even we were not able to recognize the steep turns on the road.

"Keep driving fast Avi. Don't let them take another chance" shouted Nischay.

"You don't worry dude, I know the tactics to dodge the fuckers" I replied in firm confidence.

We were able to dupe them after making five or six sharp turns. After a non-stop drive of ten minutes we reached the main road.

A lot of thoughts about our rescue were running in our minds.

"Dude we did it!" said Nischay in a joyous voice.

We drove back to Nischay's place.

"Avi and Nischay a virtual synonym of records and feats in the arena of presence of mind, have again done wonders in their characteristic style" said Nischay loudly.

'Saale kachhe khiladi the!', I laughed. We were celebrating our successful rescue.

It was quite incredible for us to reach back safely. We were thankful to god who surely helped us in making full use of our reflexes.

The next morning I kept sitting for sometime drinking milk and pondering about the strange thing that had happened. My dad often says "When you want something truly by heart, all the universe conspires in helping you to achieve it." Neha this is not the English version of the dialogue used by *Shahrukh* in *Om Shanti Om*, he actually motivates me by saying that.

And the very incident proved it to the fullest. While facing them we had nothing in our mind but to dupe them and run away.

I returned back home at seven in the morning. Dad had just finished watering the lawn, so it was cool and fragrant outside. *"Beta, dinner pe gaye the ya hotel banane?"* he asked.

"Kal Nischay ke yaha hee so gaya tha papa" I said in a sleepy tone.

Then I went straight to my room and rested for two hours. Mom woke me up at for breakfast. I enjoyed the delicious *paranthas* and *aloo ki sabzi*. I got ready and went to office by eleven. Our office is a fascinating one, especially from the day when Bhayia got its interior changed. I snuck into Pa's cabin and hung around waiting for him to look at me, because in the morning I had not met him properly. But he was busy talking to some dealer on phone.

I went on a round to the office to meet the staff.

"Hello Mohanji. How's everything going?"

"Sab badiya sir" he replied.

"Aap kab aaye?" Bhojakji asked.

"Bas Bhojakji, aaj subah hee!"

I saw the go-down filled up with stock of home theatres and music systems. It excited me as I had never seen them before in the office. I didn't knew that Pa took their agency too. I rushed back to his cabin. He was still on the phone.

"Papa" I shouted but in a low voice.

He looked at me, smiled and hung off.

"Arrey, when did you come to the office? And by the way when are you planning to go? Today?"

"No Pa....Yes Pa. College are already open. Attendance short ho jayegi....." I said in a dull but explanatory voice.

"What time is your bus?"

"Ten at night Papa"

"Go and tell your mom that we are going out for dinner today"
"Okay papa" I said beaming happily.

Flying
high

"Hi" Lisha greeted me with a warm hug and a kiss on my left cheek, which sounded like *puchhhh*!

I smiled. I bought two tickets of the back seats. It supposed to be a great lonely place in the night journey via a bus. The bus departed from ISBT Delhi at around ten thirty. We were arranging ourselves till we crossed Delhi. I was actually trying to avoid the crowded part of our journey. I wanted to be with her when no one was around. We wrapped ourselves in the quilt she carried.

We started confessing how much we missed each other. We started talking all the stuff we had stored in the last few days. I narrated the Nahargarh story. She felt nervous about it and hugged me. "Avi, why do you try risky adventure? Is it necessary?" she asked in sweet but sad voice. I remained silent. I promised her not to repeat the same in future. I was actually feeling a sense of responsibility then.

Neha, it has been truly said that a girl changes your life completely. Just imagine that while trying newest adventures I had never felt before the responsibilities towards my family, my mom and dad, bhayia and bhabhi, Tinni. I had never thought that any damage to me can create havocs at home. Thankfully I realized it then. But the credit goes to Lisha. Her care and sweetness forced me feel the duties and responsibilities deeply.

I placed my hand on her shoulder and gently stroked it. She didn't push it away. I let it travel and felt the softness of her ear and pushed my fingers through the locks of her hair. She lowered her eyes. I kissed on her forehead and said "I am proud to have you in my life Lisha Ma'am". She opened her eyes wide. It seemed as if something had annoyed her. I didn't know what. "Am I still your ma'am? We are friends now so please stop catting me that." she said in a voice that sounded a bit irritated.

"I am sorry ma'am" I said and made the blunder again.

But this time we laughed. We were getting into a state of perpetual giggling.

The journey went on with more discussions. We were getting closer and closer. We had disclosed almost all the secrets of our lives. She could make me forget the surroundings. I was completely lost in her now. Yes, I was in love. But it was too early to confess to her. To be true I didn't have the guts to propose to her formally. The time passed on with our non-stop talks. She laughed at all my weird jokes and even I did the same. There was nothing on which we didn't share a heavy laugh. We were enjoying each others company. After four-five hours of the most distinguished talks we started feeling tired and sleepy. But we didn't want to miss a single moment of the delicacy of this time. So we continued till next thirty minutes. Then I requested her to take rest. She agreed taking a deep breath. She put her hand around my waist and fell on my shoulder.

I covered her completely with the quilt. I couldn't see even a tiny particle disturbing her. She folded her legs and leaned completely on me. I put my hand from her back on her shoulder and held her tightly. I kept looking at her. She looked like a small innocent school going kid. That sight of hers carried all the sweetness, all the beauty god has ever produced on earth.

We reached Doon at five in the morning. Lisha was still asleep. I didn't want to wake her up, I wanted time to freeze. But the bus had stopped, so we were supposed to get off.

"Good morning Lisha ma'am..... Lisha" I corrected myself. My fingers were still on her cheeks.

"Good morning Smartie".

I loved the way she had started greeting me.

"Hmmmm.....then?" asked Neha.

"If I believe I cannot do something, it makes me incapable of doing it. But when I believe I can, than I acquire the ability to do it even if I didn't have it in the beginning" was said by Mahatma Gandhi. I practised the same in all the phases of my 24 years life.

On 8th October 2003, I took a decision to go for uniting a team and organizing ourselves into a professional club. What should be the basic objective of the club? What must be its name? Who all should I choose as a powerful team? How should I give a start to my first dream, after taking admission into the Bachelor of Technology course? , etc were some of the questions which kept juggling in my mind until the final day arrived..........

The night out at cafeteria, DIT on 24 Nov'03 was the most memorable hang out with my friends. For one, it gave us ARDC. And two, it is not everyday you sit along with your friends and discuss your future very seriously. *High dreams, great aspirations, zeal and enthusiasm to reach all impossible heights were the burning discussion of that night.*

Yes, you see it in movies, you hear stories from your friends about such groups but it never happens to you. *It happened with us......*

Aditya, DC, Sumit, Ashish, Piyush, Ntini, Jatin and I, were the ones who decided to spend out our night in the TT Hall above cafeteria.

We used to den their many a times but this time it *was different*!!! With coffee mugs and maggi bowls in hand we started with the very distinguished talk.

"I dream of becoming a tycoon in automobile industry. I aspire of owning my own automobile firm which will aid clients with the gadgets of their own choice.", DC started, "I want to bring a revolution in beaurocracy, I want to be at the top and guys you know what, am going to outsmart the current system very soon," I added.

"*O really*', Jatin interrupted, 'C'mon guys talk something senseful, something which can be applied on us at the moment. I want fame in our institute, in India and all over the world!" "Everybody wants to…….but how," added Ashish.

We stayed quiet for a minute.

"Let me say something on this score," I said.

"Friends, the longest journey begins with the single first step," I added, just to break the silence.

"Success can only come to you by courageous devotion to the task lying in front of you," said Ntini.

"See, that makes me uncomfortable. I want to achieve heights at the earliest by hook or crook." said Piyush.

"Yes, that's very true. We must plan out Suez banks robbery!" laughed Sumit at him.

"To achieve success, ensure progress, and gain fame, one has to take risks, we must not miss the opportunity and take inspiration from the movie *The Italian Job*," suggested Piyush.

"Dude, think in right direction. There is no shortcut or magic formula to get famous, all we need to do is to believe in ourselves. Think something constructive, something on which we can feel proud upon." I said in a firm voice.

"I agree, I guess we should start up as a team and work on some project, completion of which will take our name to each corner of the campus," said Aditya adding gravity to my point.

'Friends, let us take all the aspects into concern and then plan a club which will work accordingly. Technical, literary and cultural skills should be developed so that we can produce dynamic personalities.' I said. Everybody was listening carefully to me. We then shifted our den to boys' hostel's terrace and the discussion continued till next morning, we had to miss our classes as we didn't bothered to see the clock.

A flood of thought and images swam in my mind the whole day.

We were all thrilled with the ideas that we shared. In the evening we introduced our planning to Manpreet, JK, Rohit, Varun & Ishaan, some of our day-scholar mates.

They gave a spark to the plan of forming a club.

'Recreation & Hobby Club should be the name of our club', said JK smashing his hand on the cafeteria's side platforms.

Ishan, Varun, Manpreet & Aditya threw a disgusting glance at JK. "Guys, we are going to work for the development of our resources, so think something which relates to it." said Rohit.

"It's name should be ALL-ROUND DEVELOPMENT CLUB.", said Manpreet.

"All Round Development Club...." Sumit and DC repeated, giving a deep thought to it.

"And how does that justify to our objectives?" asked Varun.

Manpreet explained it well. Aditya and DC supported Manpreet's suggestion and added up points for the very name.

We all agreed!!

The idea was discussed with Dean Academics who granted his full support for the functioning of the club in the institute. With lots of suggestions and ideas from him and Dean Students Welfare, we stood as a team and inaugurated our club on 3 Feb'04.

On the inaugural day, we disclosed the vision and the objectives of the club to the students and faculties. "ARDC visions to instill in each student those qualities of mind and character necessary for good citizenship and dynamic leadership including broad technical and cultural curiosity that embraces open-mindedness with creative thinking.", said I. JK, Varun & Rohit then displayed the working model on "Train Simulator" which was followed by launching of our website, **www.ardcdit.com**. The inspiring words of Director, Dean Academics and other faculty members helped us in galvanizing our thoughts.

Seven days later we came up with 'HORIZON-04, an intra-college fest', which had events related to technical, cultural and literary activities and sports. The events were one of their own kinds. Attracting students to participate was a difficult job and we were overwhelmed to have a participation of more than 1000 students, which was three times more than expected. *Yes, it was a big success...* and the first milestone for our club to work with same enthusiasm and creativity.

I suggested to all those who approached us that "Whatever you can do or dream you can, begin it. Boldness has genius, power and magic in it. Begin it now."

'You have done a great job and really succeeded in your objective of developing resources, indirectly you have achieved the target. Your energetic initiative has given a platform to a number of Student Activity Club(s). Great going.......' said Dean Academics, who was the pillar of strength behind us.

That was how the team of thirteen came up as Founder Chairpersons of a multi-dimensional club. ARDC became a part of my life. We organized a number of events in the college. Whatever we had achieved was because a few ordinary people who got together, believed in the dream of achieving extra-ordinary things.

Engineers Day, Founders Day, Convocation Ceremony, Farewell Party were amongst the great hit events organized by us. All the events were a roaring success, much beyond what we had expected. My team continued to organize such mega-busters. Teachers Day, Independence Day, Sports Week, Theme Cultural Nights, etc were all consecutively organized and headed by me. It tested my organizational skills to the utmost and I was quite satisfied with the way we had managed academics in parallel with so much of extra co-curricular activities.

Seeing my incredible performance I was selected the Vice-President of Indian Society for Technical Education, DIT Chapter. I became an instant celebrity the college campus and my entire friend circle. Most importantly, it gave a boost to my confidence in my ideas and abilities. In that time I had a real passion for filling up the gaps. My sole ambition was to give an elegant performance.

Into the
stormy waters

Neha I forgot to tell you one most tragic incidents that actually changed my life. Let us enter into a little flash back.

It was 24th November'03, we had internal practical exams in the college. The college staff got us engaged till the evening. I had to miss lunch. Late in the evening I was called for the viva. It was really tragic to face technical bouncers when you are totally exhausted. It was all a mess. My answers were like answers by a moron.

I returned to the hostel and slept off.

"Avi it is ten now! Have you had your dinner?" enquired a senior residing in the same corridor I was.

"No Sir, I was very tired so just slept off. But am feeling very hungry now." I replied.

"Dude, all the stores are closed today. No cafeteria, no Nescafe!", he sympathized.

"Oh! That's unfair. I am dying of hunger. I need to eat something." I cried.

"Stop behaving like a kid and let us find out something." he suggested.

We flopped into each and every room just to find out if there was something to eat. But alas! We didn't find even a couple of biscuits. That very day I realised the value of food. I was literally starving. During while my search for food I encountered Aditya on the fourth floor of the Boys Hostel Block II. Aditya was a very genuine, sincere and a decent chap. We loved calling him Aditya Sirjee. He was a Mechanical Engineering student and a very good friend of mine. Aditya and I had been apartment mates in the first year of our hostel stay. I remember the fun we used to have in apartment no. 408.

Well, let me not digress from the topic and tell you about that desperate night. So, when I was exhausted searching for food. Aditya gave me the idea to cross the college boundaries and go to the railway station. The railway station is the only place in Doon where you can find vendors open for all 24 hours.

"But we don't have an outpass baby!" I said.

"Ya that's true." said Aditya. "We have only two options left." he added.

"And what are they?"

"The first is to get out of the gate anyhow."

"And whats the second one?" I asked.

"To go back to bed and wait for tomorrow!" he sniggered.

I felt like giving a tight punch on his maxillae. I was not at all enjoying his jokes. I had one thing in my mind and that was to cross the college boundary in any case. I am not a person who gives up, at least not without waging a war. I contacted some of my seniors for the same. Kandy Sir, Monk Sir, Roy Sir and Pranjil Sir felt the urgency I had. They agreed to accompany me. We arranged 3 bikes.

A blue Pulsar, a Unicorn and a black Pulsar took all six of us to the railway station. At the college main gate we convinced the guards to allow us to go for half an hour. They agreed!

The lonely road, the whispering of trees and ice-chilled breeze created a feeling of extraordinary thrill. We were speeding at between 80-90 Km/Hr. The winters here in Doon are really freezing ones. Temperature falls to 3 degrees. The fog is so dense as if the fronts of Owashio and Kuroshio currents have shifted from Japan to the Doon valley. It completely disables visibility.

"Kandy Sir, drive slowly! Nothing is visible to me." I shouted. Don't worry dude! Pranjil is heading above 100" he replied. "God damm! Who is gonna stop these guys?" said Aditya.

I was a bit tense about the way we came out of the college. And the way the seniors were driving. I was continuously giving them the instructions to drive safe.

They were least bothered about it. I kept trying to catch them. But I couldn't make it as they had crossed 100.

"What if warden comes on for a check?" "What if the guards inform about us?" "What if we don't reach back on time?" a plethora of such questions rattled me, often leading to momentary lapses in concentration. One such lapse had Roy Sir skip my indications at Malsi Deer Park.

The bike that Roy Sir was driving swerved dangerously. "Oh Shit!" said Kandy Sir. "Oh no Brother!" erupted Aditya with excessive force. Something obviously very wrong had happened, I sensed.

Both Roy Sir and Pranjil Sir screeched to a halt, a chill ran down their spines. I could not believe what I saw in front of my eyes, Pranjil Sir was lying unconscious in a pool of blood with a deep cut on his shoulder.

We thanked God that he was still alive, but Roy Sir and his bike were nowhere to be seen.

The city was still 10 kilometers away and it was impossible to get any help at that hour on an ice-chilling night.

We realized that Pranjil Sir was bleeding profusely from the wound on his shoulder and needed the medical assistance quickly. Monk Sir and I started looking for the bike and Roy Sir and we found him unconscious in the bushes along the road.

He was breathing but the pulse was very low. It looked as if they had tried to turn too quickly and the bike skidded. Pranjil Sir had landed on his shoulder and was knocked out but Roy Sir got entangled with the bike.

Aditya managed to stop the highway patrol car and get both to the nearest hospital quickly. Both of them were quickly attended, Pranjil Sir had a minor injury but Roy Sir's condition worsened.

He had lost a lot of blood and it was impossible to find a blood bank or a donor at this time. But, it was lucky for us that Kandy Sir and I had the same blood group (A+) as him. The doctor assured us of his stabilized condition in a few hours. We leaved a breath of relief.

Back in college, I climbed up the stairs, fumbling with the lock of my room when I heard some students talking about the disciplinary action to be taken against the students who had gone out the last night.

I tensed instinctively.

The very next moment I hurled Aditya's door open, holding the lock and keys in one hand. "Hey Aditya, they are going to expel us." I yelled.

"What! How come they know about it?"

"There must be some traitor among us. I guess we should go and tell them the truth before they take up their own decision." I suggested.

"Let me think about it." he yelled back.

"What the hell for? They have issued the notice *damm-it!*"

Aditya chortled "C'mon dude, don't worry. They won't be treating us in such a harsh way. The notice is just to scare us."

"I hope that the Director and Dean cooperates." I said.

"They are very friendly. They will definitely understand the issue." said Aditya in a very assuring way.

"Yeah, but not always. Wait till they call back once, you'd think you'd murdered their wife, the way they carry on."

My cell phone rang at this point.

"Hello. Is this Avinash Jain?" asked a firm voice.

"Yes. Who's this?" I asked.

"PA to Director, DIT. You have been expelled from the hostel with immediate effect. Kindly receive the notice."

I couldn't go on. I hung up. I needed some time to absorb that shock. I knew it was on the cards but I still needed time. My mind jutted into the past. How it had come to that. How an easy and satisfied life had gotten sour.

The hostel warden walked in and said, "Management wants to see you guys in the Director's cabin immediately."

"We are coming." I said.

I was surprised and pained. I asked him the reason of such a strict disciplinary action, to which he said "You have been charged for drinking while driving, making a forged out-pass and not informing the college authority about the accident," "You must check out the notice." he added.

Aditya and I rushed to the college notice board. I spent fifteen minutes gazing at the notice for us. I saw my name announcing the immediate expulsion. I marched along the corridor, with a pre-occupied look, to the college reception.

"Avi and Aditya," said the Dean setting himself on the sofa in the Director's room, "I am very disappointed. I never expected this from you."

"The charges against you are forcing us to expel you from the hostel" added Director Sir.

"Sir, may I please know what are the charges against me?" I burst out in anger.

"You were found drunk. You forged an out-pass. You were speeding on the road." shouted one of the members of the Discipline Committee.

I couldn't understand a word of what he said, but could sense the rage and hatred which spewed out of his mouth like a tangible flame. I stood quiet and listened to it all. I will never forget that meeting in which I was literally humiliated. I had never expected such a treatment from the college management. They made me feel as if I had committed a rape or a murder kind of thing.

But a blunder is a blunder whether small or big, today I realise.

"We'd like to see your parents tomorrow morning." said the Director.

They left us with no options but to call up our parents. Aditya's parents had gone to Kolkata for some family function so it was not possible for them to come. I called up home and in a single breath vomitted out the complete matter.

"What? What are you talking about?" Dad sounded angry, anxious, affectionate, all at the same time. The moment I heard his voice, I felt terribly homesick. I knew exactly where he was standing, near the dining table in the center hall, speaking on the cordless phone. Dadiji would be sleeping in Tinni's room, and Dad would be trying to keep his voice down so that Mom didn't sense the trouble.

"Dad, I'm sorry, I'm sorry, I'm fine. Please don't worry but come here otherwise they are going to expel me tonight." I said.

Dad said something in reply and hung up. I couldn't catch his words, I was too nervous. Feeling extremely ashamed, I walked to my room.

I had thought that Mom & Dad would be angry. Say hard things and hit their forehead on the wall. But they were so wonderfully peaceful.

They boarded the direct bus from Jaipur to Dehradun at 4:00 pm the same day and reached next morning.

I touched the feet of Mom and Dad and begged pardon for my misconduct. I showed them the notice which had been issued against me and which had the charges of drinking, signing a forged out-pass and driving unsafe.

Tear drops trickled like pearls down Mom's cheeks, wetting the Notice. For a moment she closed her eyes and then hugged me. I too broke down.

"Avi, we know that you do not drink. Also, we know that you won't ever attempt to sign a forged out-pass" said Dad.

"So, no need to worry. We will talk to the authorities."

"Now will you take us to your room or do you want us to meet the Dean here?" Dad smiled.

I took the luggage and we went to my room in the hostel. I collapsed on my bed, trying to cover my head with my pillow. I had a headache. After about an hour we headed to talk to the management. We waited at the reception to talk directly to the Vice-Chairman first. It was more than four hours before he called us in. Dad asked me to wait outside. I was feeling very bad about what was happening.

After about five minutes, Mom & Dad came out without a positive output. By that time Aditya came with his local guardians. All six of us went inside the Director's room.

"Welcome, Mr. & Mrs. Jain." greeted the Director.

Director Sir made our parents comfortably seated. We were standing near the door of the room.

"Sir, I have heard to the whole story from my son. Expel my boy as per your decision but we want you to allow him to stay in the hostel for the next twenty days, so that his final exams get over." requested my father.

"Sir, we have already taken the decision and it cannot be changed at any case." Director Sir replied.

"But Sir, you must at least think before taking such a harsh decision." Mom said angrily.

"Mrs. Jain we understand your concern but your child must have given a thought before committing such a heinous crime. Now it is not in our hand." The Director said. "Mrs. Jain, a panel of six senior members of the college management has decided this." he justified.

The justification of the Director had given a slight idea to Mom & Dad that I had committed something serious. Their anger against the college authority went down.

"Sir, we are not asking you to cancel your decision but just postpone it." said Dad.

"Where are these boys going to stay?" "I mean they need some time to search an accommodation" said Mom. "At least excuse them till their exams get over." she added.

"We are sorry Ma'am." he answered.

Dean Sir entered.

"*Aa gaye aap log.* Nice to see you." said the Dean to our parents.

"*Aap hee samjhaiye Sir.*" said Director to the Dean.

"Ma'am we have no personal grudge against your sons. But he and his friends have committed such a crime which can not to be taken lightly at any cost." said the Dean.

My parents remained silent. They must be thinking of the gravity of the crime we had committed. They must have wondered at the words Dean was using against us. Crime!!!

Neha you tell me, was going out to get something to eat a Crime? Was calling a Doctor and Police at the accident spot a Crime? Was donating blood to the victims a Crime? Was returning to the hostel and telling the true story a Crime?

"Sir, please try to understand. My child is innocent." requested Mom.

"If it was all so innocent, why did you not come directly to us?" The

Dean burst on us. *"Aaj ham aur aap milke aapke bachhe to thappar nai maarenge to kal duniya inhe maaregi."* he shouted.

His pinching words humiliated me and Mom & Dad. He requested us to leave and not buy time on this issue. "They are not telling you the truth, they have committed a blunder I tell you." he said.

Aditya and I were thinking of some excuse. I was about to say something but the Dean seemed to have an incredible ability to read a student's mind. "Don't try to bring up new situations." he shouted.

"Sorry Sir. I accept your decision." a murmured voice. Mom shook her head in disbelief.

We went out.

The next morning when I woke up, my head felt as if India and U.S were exchanging nuclear fuel inside its. I staggered out of bed, stumbled to the bathroom. Sweating and panting, I groped my way back to the bed and lay there gasping.

My breathing began to ease and I started feeling much better. The nuclear deal inside the cerebrum had subsided, but an active insurgency still seemed under way, characterized by a nearly continuous burst of machine-gun fire across the centre of my head.

I was wrestling with myself when I walked out of my room and headed for the campus. Mom, Dad and Aditya accompanied me.

We found notices of our expulsion placed on every notice board that came across. We took our leave from the college.

After visualizing the consequences of their decision I broke down. How will things get managed? How was I going to appear for my external exams? Where am I going to make my stay?

I never cried from the day I had gained my senses. I never cried even when I got badly burnt on Diwali. I never cried when I had a fight with my closest friends. I never cried when Mom and Dad didn't allow me to join the Indian Air Force. But that day, when I was expelled, I cried and cried.

Dad held me and let me use his shirt to wipe away my tears.

"Avi, stop behaving like a kid." Aditya said.

He'd never seen me like that. But it happens when you suffer unnecessarily. That was unfair. Someone out in the management needed to realize that keeping those who were the main culprits inside the hostel and throwing us out was completely unfair.

Mom's eyes were full of tears and so were mine. I was expelled out from the hostel with immediate effect. An air of curiosity spread in the hostel, like forest fire. I had to vacate my room the very next day. I assured mom and dad that I had made all the arrangements at my friend's place, so there was no need to worry. I would take care of everything, I assured them.

"A sudden setback can be seen as a brick wall. It can also be seen as a stepping stone" Dad said.

"*Beta* don't worry at all. Your parents are with you. Let us know if you find any difficulty outside"

Dad always visualizes my situation by putting himself in my shoes. He is always there for me. I remember a short story about a child and a father and I would like to narrate it to tell you the role my parents play in my life.

A city faced a severe cyclone. Thousands of people died when buildings fell on them. People were running here and there to save their lives. A father and a child were also running to find shelter. On the way there was a bridge to be crossed to reach the safe end. The father asked the child to hold him tightly so that he could try crossing the bridge. The child said "Father, I won't hold your hand," he requested his father to hold his hand tightly as he feared that in a difficult situation he might leave his father's hand but however bad condition might be, his father could never leave him till the end.

So that is the role our parents play into our life. I was happy that my parents stood firmly with me giving me a moral support. They taught me to face failures and disappointments without feeling defeated.

But I could sense their agony. If I were a painter I could draw a picture of the whole scene today. It is still so vivid in my mind. Those pearl drops of love cleansed my heart, and washed my sin away. Only someone who ever has experienced such love can know what it is.

Aditya and I packed our bags and left the hostel the same day in the evening.

We had final examinations of fourth semester looming close. It was not feasible for us to find a good accommodation in the city in such a short period of time.

Sometimes life takes so many turns that we loose our will to combat them. But a setback is not final by itself. It is instead, an opportunity to learn, improve and move on. During that stage, I had gone through many ups and downs, many successes and failures. I learnt from failures and hardened myself with courage to face them.

For the first three-four days, Lisha was not ready to believe that I had been expelled. Gradually she realized the truth of the decision. Daily she used to ask me about if something could be done regarding this matter. She remained tensed 24 * 7.

"How is it possible that nothing can be done?" Lisha called. She got irritated at the way the management of the college behaved in handling my case. She got totally disappointed. "So where are you going to stay?" she asked.

"Dear please don't panic na. There are many of my friends outside, I'll confirm it by evening" I assured her.

The clock showed three in the afternoon.

Aditya and I went to Chachu's place. Chachu had been our apartment mate in the Hostel Block III in the first year of our engineering.

He was delighted to see us.

"*Aao Shero aao*" he greeted us. "I have made all the arrangements for your stay. But there is a problem as you can see it is a *gaon*. Only two things you will have to manage, one there is shortage of electricity at night and second you will have to burn sticks to boil water".

"We will adjust" I said. Aditya was looking around, perhaps he was checking the rest of the facilities at our accommodation.

"Oh you are standing" Chachu cried, picking a chair from the verandah outside.

"No. No don't trouble yourself. I can sit on the floor" I said.

I received the chair but gently passed it to Aditya and sat on the floor.

"Thank you brother for your support. I hope we are not troubling you" Aditya completed the formalities.

Formalities because what could be done even if Chachu got troubled? Would Aditya leave the place? So what was the point of thanking. But, dignity demands it be done.

"Ya you are troubling me" he replied and a seconds pause followed and then we all laughed. It was the first time after the confirmation of our expulsion that I laughed joyously.

We unloaded our luggage.

The fight for our semesters then started........................

Lisha used to call me at 11:30 at night. The first twenty-thirty minutes she used to pep me up. Then she used to tell me the important topics to be studied, one by one of all the subjects. She always reminded me of the external papers and worked day and night to help me out in my studies. I actually started taking tele-tuitions.

We used to talk till five in the morning. It was so lovely to talk into the night with her. It became our habit to study on phone. I had no other option left. Before falling asleep, she used to hug me and kiss me as like muuaahh, mmmmmuuuaaahh and then say "Avi, you have to do well, never loose hope".

Her supporting nature and caring words used to give me strength. Daily we used to meet and study together till her in-time of hostel. We often had our lunch together. Sometimes we would go to the *dhabas,* sometimes to the college-cafeteria and sometimes to the city.

We also went to Shiv Mandir on alternate days. That was the place where I used to relax. Lisha used to look directly into my eyes and give her most beautiful smile.

"Everything that happens is for the good" she used to say. We used to take a walk around the perimeter of the temple and discuss the syllabus to be covered, the strategy of studying. She used to boost my moral, she used to support me in every way she could.

One evening we took a long walk past the DIT property and down the tree-lined road. Each time my feet hit the ground a voice in my brain went "don't panic, don't panic" in an insanely rhythm.

"Why are you silent Avi? *Ab kya hua?*" she asked.

I was standing expressionless, like a body without soul.

She hugged me.

That evening I was not silent because of the bad time I was facing but because I was admiring the purity and beauty of the sweetest girl I had ever seen in my life. Yes, I am talking about Lisha only. She was looking drop-dead gorgeous as usual. Her hair were super-straight, her clingy clothes were in yummy ice-cream colors and, as she enveloped me in a massive hug, I discovered that she smelled divine.

I too grabbed her in my arms, "Thanks for everything Lisha".

"No need to mention. It's completely my pleasure"

Everything was turning so beautiful with her presence around me.

I found myself studying late in the library, sometimes till the morning. It was not because I enjoyed it but I had to, to at least score the passing marks. And to prove myself to the college management that I was not amongst those who they thought of. I devoted my energy completely for scoring a good percentage in the externals.

At night the tears would stream down my cheeks, and home memories of all sorts made sleep out of the question. It was impossible to share my misery with anyone. And even if I would have done so, where was the use? I knew of nothing that would soothe me. Everything was strange. I was a complete novice in the matter and continually had to be on my guard. But Chachu used to give all kindness and attention. He treated us as his own brothers.

"I am so glad you guys are here with me" I cried, swooping down and squeezing Chachu and Aditya together into a big group hug.

"Chal ab senti mat kar yaar, go and take rest" Chachu said.

Suddenly loud shout erupted from then nearby room. Panicking, we looked wildly around for something with which to defend ourselves. Nobody had been in the room when we had left it. For us it was some unthinkable horror. Perhaps some ghost that hated our presence. Visions from the '*Hills Have Eyes*' which we had seen at hostel dripped like cold blood from our veins into the cerebrum.

'*Come here darling*' whooshed a voice in the next room. There was something hypnotic about that voice. Aditya stilled his pounding heart. Nobody had emerged from the room. Picking up the kitchen knife I crept to the door and flung it open. There wasn't a soul, the windows were still shut. Aditya strode furiously towards Jaggi, Chachu's room mate, as soon as he saw him coming. "There was somebody" he complained.

"Where?" asked he.

"There inside the room. He was calling us darling......may be a ghost" shivered Aditya.

'Oh Sorry',said he contritely. "Did that scare you? I was taming a dog at the backyard. It was just me dude. Just chill." explained he to us.

We felt relieved.

"I hope you guys are comfortable here" he enquired.

"Ya we are" I assured. We went to bed.

The next morning Chachu arrived and taught us the process of boiling water for bath. He collected some wood sticks and put them in the *Choolah,* poured kerosene and lit them on.

A glance at the door showed there was no way to lock it. I peered outside but no inspiration rounded the corner. I looked around inside but nothing presented itself that could be used to jam the door. Suddenly remembering, I dashed to the soap wrappers lying inside the bathroom, folded them quickly into a square and stuffed it under the corner of the door. Still I was not able to manage it properly. "Fear not fair youth, I shall stand guard outside and none shall witness the noble nakedness, as Shakespeare probably said" giggled Aditya.

I undressed to take bath. I was soaping myself all over when I suddenly noticed that the door wide open.

Aditya was watching me very calmly. "Shut the door, asshole." I urged.

"I think it would be nice to be gay." he said.

(Neha laughed)

With the help of the bucket I protected the censored body parts and rushed to shut the door. Aditya was too much! We were able to adjust with lifestyle of the place but the tensions of the examinations coming dawned in me.

When every hope is gone, 'when helpers fail and comforts flee', I find that help in some or the other form arrives, from I know not where. This time it came in the form of extreme love and affection from Lisha.

Lisha used to be in touch with me twenty-four hours. She kept pepping me up. She used to teach me on phone continuously for hours. Though Lisha was my senior and not even part of the same stream, she used to study my subjects first from her friends and then explain them to me. Lisha was unusual in her own way.

Early in the morning when I used to go back to the room after spending whole night in the library, she used to wave to me from the girls hostel's balcony.

I remember it was 14th December, early in the morning, Aditya and I were returning to our room from the library. While we were crossing the Girls Hostel, my phone rang.

It was Lisha's call.

"Avi meet me behind the nescafe right now." and she disconnected.

She gave me no time to think of what the reason for this could be. Instantly I had to rush. I asked Aditya to wait there and watch out for the guards till I returned.

I reached the back of the Nescafe kiosh and found her sitting on a stone.

"What are you doing here Cheeku?" I asked.

"Just wanted to see you Avi."

"Have you gone crazy? Lisha you know what you have done. If you're caught, they will expel you too."

"No one knows about it. I know a *chor-raasta*. I will be back in my room in fifteen minutes. And waise I'll love to be expelled, *ham saath mei rahenge*"

Her answer forced me to think about my identity. She was far more brave and bold than I was in playing with the restrictions. I mean this is expected from the boys, I guess. In our case it was just the opposite, She actually possessed bold and courageous genes. Huh... I was surprised how she could do so.

"You are managing it rather well Avi, I am proud of you." she said in a whisper.

"Lisha, after five hours I have my paper. I just don't know what I am going to attempt. EMI is so damm difficult." I said nervously.

"Avi, just stop thinking about the paper now." she said in typical Lisha style.

I nodded but I had wet eyes which clearly depicted the tension in my mind.

She came close to me and held my hand. I was still tense about the paper.

She came even closer then. The gap reduced to zero. I don't know who initiated it. I felt something warm on my lips, we kept kissing each other.

96

It was one of the most wonderful times I had in my life. Kissing my love early in the morning behind the Nescafe kiosh was unimaginable! Then I could believe that whatever happened was for the good of me.

Imagine, I started believing my expulsion from the hostel to be a good decision. Had I not been expelled, it could never have happened. I was thankful to my destiny.

After about two hundred seconds, we stopped. She smiled and ran away without saying a word.

I kept looking at her. She turned back, smiled and then again turned and headed for the *chor-raasta*.

Aditya popped in.

"Hmmmm…. Avi what is the matter? I guess something fishy is happening" he smiled.

"Nothing dude. She was just wishing me good luck." I replied knowing that it would not work in killing Aditya's curiosity.

Well, we headed for our room. I was amazed at the way in which the things were moving. We were in love.

One night at Roxberry

The fourth semester was the most fantastic period of my college life. Three big things happened one after the other. One, I cleared the third semester papers with aggregate of 69.8. Second Lisha and I came closer and third I had executed my plans and goals successfully.

On weekends we found ourselves hanging out for some movie or the other. I remember we used to see eight-ten movies a month. We used to repeat many of them. I remember once when there was no movie left to see, we bought tickets for Jai Santoshi Maa. Not because we were religious kind of but because we needed time to spend together and the movie halls were the only place in Doon where I could manage to hide my face from work.

While the other fellows in the hall used to enjoy the movie, I used to tease Lisha, I never let her watch the movie. She used to get annoyed many times but I was not amongst the one who would agree to her request. *Only the idiots of highest order would concentrate on the movie, while on a date,* I used to enjoy the other film.

Months passed and our bonding grew stronger and stronger.

In the college, I remained devoted myself to my work. I had always managed my work, my studies and the fun well. The leisure I took out from my schedule solved the purpose of all the *masti* I indulged in. Often my juniors asked me about my time management tactics. "Sir, how do you manage your engineering study, the civil services preparation, the extra and co-curricular, the president-ship of so many societies and the *masti*. You even go to Gym na? How do you do that?", "Sir, how do you take out time for Lisha Ma'am?" and even my classmates asked, "How are you handling all this Avi?", and to all their questions I had only one answer that *busy is a person who has time for everything.*

ARDC was attaining heights. People started calling us ARDCians. We were allowed to meet the senior administering staff directly, without taking any permissions and appointments. We enjoyed our status in college.

Many students used to approach me for joining ARDC. But our policies were yet not open for the others to join. The frequent requests made us conduct a meeting of the 13 jumbos!

"We must open the doors of our club for others to join." started Manpreet.

"Not a great idea. Are 13 of us incompetent?" said Jatin.

"Fairly not. But to expand we need to spread our wings" said DC.

"And memberships would help us in increasing funds of the club too." Aditya added.

The meeting went on for an hour wherein we discussed all the pros and cons of opening membership. We moved ahead with the idea. We decided the terms and conditions, eligibility, the categories and the hierarchy to be followed. The opening of membership resulted to be the turning point in the working methodology of ARDC.

We divided ourselves to fill the posts. A hierarchy was to be followed for proper decentralization of powers. We elected the President, Vice-President, Technical Head, Literary Head, Cultural Head, Treasurer and Auditor, as each one of was equally competent for all the posts.

Well, I got diverted. Sorry Neha but I don't want any story to be left untold. Anyways lets get back onto the track, Lisha truly supported me for my hard work and devotion to all the activities I had initiated. She was never annoyed with my busy schedule. It happened when for the days we did not meet each other but just talked on the phone in the evening for a couple of minutes. And it worked well in maintaining our relationship.

One day I remember, I called up all my friends to join the hang out at my place at night. Obviously the female ones were not to be invited for a night stay but truly speaking I wanted them to be present. After all they add decency and glamour to the get-togethers. So, the male members of ARDC team gathered in the evening to celebrate the success of ARDC.

With coke cans and *bhujia* we started off with our very exclusive discussion. One thing I would like to mention about my group is that we always discussed something that resulted in some constructive output. We talked about development, about problems in the society, about politics as well as the politicians. We talked about ideas, we worked on solutions. This was how we worked and planned.

"Guys, my motive of calling you all here was not just to celebrate but to plan out the calendar for the next semester." I stood up and said.

"*Yaar aaj to maaf karde.*" Ntini said.

"*Duniya sudhar jayegi par ye nai sudhrega.*" I heard it from someone in the group.

"We are all together after a long gap. And ARDCians always get grouped for some good cause." I reminded him.

"You are a real diplomat." DC appreciated.

"Okay, let us begin with a soft-drink cheer." Manpreet said. And we clanked our soft-drink mugs with a loud cheer.

And the talks proceeded.

We started planning for a three day inter-college fest in the college. The events, the organizing team, the budget, the sponsors, the utilization of infrastructure, expected gathering, the marketing team and every related issue were discussed. It struck two and we were still busy finalizing the proposal for the fest and sports week.

"All the three days would be followed by cultural nights." Manpreet suggested.

"Even DJ's should be included." Rohit said.

"We will call Sonu Nigam for the cultural night." Piyush said.

"To hell with Nigam. I am feeling hungry. Is there something to eat?" JK demanded.

And all of a sudden the discussion diverted. Actually we had worked for almost four hours, we had been speaking continuously without any input to the stomach. So, most of us were feeling hungry and sleepy. All started demanding for something to eat. But alas! All the jars were empty and all the packets of bhujia and biscuits had also been finished by the extra-enthusiastic ARDC team.

Manpreet gave us the idea of getting the mouth-watering litchis from the trees outside.

It was the last week of May and fresh season of Litchis. Litchis of Dehradun are very famous. You could see trees heavy with red juicy litchis in almost all the houses. There are big litchi farms here. Their production and farming contribute a major proportion in the exports from this state.

Aditya and I agreed to Manpreet's idea.

"Should I get litchis for everyone?" I asked, being the host of the party.

"Yes, yes we all agree." shouted JK, Piyush, Ntini and DC all together.

"Yes Yes We all agree *to aise keh rahe ho* as if you have some other option to fill your stomachs." said Aditya.

Manpreet, Aditya and I decided to go out to the street, the famous Kalidas Road, and get a hand-bag full of red-juicy litchis for everyone. "Avi, let's take a knife along with us." Manpreet suggested.

"Aditya get the torch also." I said. There were many litchi trees in our neighbourhood, so we knew that we were in for a yummy treat. We moved out, fully armed. Aditya carried the torch, Manpreet took the knife and the stick and I carried the sack for collecting the litchis. It showed 2:30 am in the clock.

It was a beautiful night. The sky was jet black. An infinite number of stars were twinkling. All three of us started betting on the constellation formation. "This is Saptarishi" shouted Aditya pointing at the question mark formed by some seven stars. "Shut Up dude, that's not Saptrishi but that's a Polar Bear" Manpreet countered. And this way our distinguished discussion began. We started talking about space science, the mythology related to it. We discussed the advancement of science in this field. ISRO, NASA, JAXA, European Space Agency were all dragged into the conversation one by one till we moved some distance away from our room.

I found that night great because here in Jaipur the glittering stars cannot be seen. Not because it is in some shadow but because of the air pollution. And not only in Jaipur, in almost all the plain areas one cannot see the beauty of stars in the sky because of the intensity of pollution covering the layer of visibility.

On our way, we kept collecting the fallen litchis. "Well, listen guys......" Aditya interrupted. "Let us start with the lowermost branches of the trees. I hope we will get enough of them." he added.

"The lower branches do not have red and the juicy ones." I said.

"But only the side and lower branches are hanging out to the street." Manpreet said.

"We are going to pluck the litchis off the trees as a team. Manpreet and I would climb up the boundary wall and from there it would be easier to pluck the red ones. You collect the ones which fall. And Aditya you help me in locating the best lot of litchis on the tree, use the torch to point them out." I declared the master plan.

"Avi look at that tree. If we can conquer it, everyone's need would be satisfied." Aditya exclaimed.

"*Dheere bol Idiot, koi uth gaya to waat lag jayegi.*" I gave a frightening stare to control his excitement.

Not wasting time, just as professionals, loaded with all the gadgets needed, we attacked the tree figured out by Aditya. And thus we started clearing the branches one by one. The divine litchis started falling. And Manpreet was busy collecting them. Three out of every ten collected ones was tasted by the three of us. We were having the greatest pleasure in eating those litchis.

We were on the eleventh boundary when we saw a two wheeler coming towards us. "Avi jump down, somebody is coming" Manpreet warned. And I jumped instantly. Manpreet quickly threw the sack, which was half full of Litchis by then, into the bushes.

We held our breath to see who it was. It was a police patrol. There were two cops on the bike doing night patrol. I immediately threw the stick tied with the knife on its upper end into the bushes and Manpreet threw the sack into the drain. Our breath started to freeze.

The policeman in the front was a well-built man close to forty, with a well grown moustache. He looked like a South-Indian villain.

"What the fuck are you doing here?" the cop asked, staring at us.

"We're just taking a walk." replied Manpreet.

"Taking a walk at 2:30 in night."

"Can't we?" I said.

"Don't utter shit or I'll screw your ass." said the inspector.

"We were just going back to our room after a walk to refresh ourselves after long hours of continuous study." said Aditya.

I could hear the pleading in Aditya's voice.

"Going back to room!" he said, after giving a pause.

"Yes Sir." Aditya nodded.

"Yes Sir!" the cop repeated. "I like that."

Both of them came near us. We felt the urge to run and hide ourselves, but our feet seemed as if they had melted in the heat and stress of the moment.

"Walk to your room right now." shouted he.

"That's what we were doing Sir." I said.

"Shut up and walk. Don't mess with me." he shouted at us again.

We started walking much faster than usual thinking that the policemen have excused us. But they were following us on their bike.

"Move faster." they shouted.

"Avi they are definitely going to ask for money" Aditya whispered.

"That would still be fine. Hope they don't smash us with their sticks"

We reached our room. The policemen came along with us into the room. Everyone was astonished.

"What happened sir?" DC enquired.

"Shut up and stand aside. All of you!" he roared.

One of them checked the whole of the room. He checked the cupboards, bed-rack, drawers, computer and toilet. The other one was standing right in front of the queue the thirteen of us had formed as per the instructions.

"Sir, will you please tell me what is going on? I mean we were just plucking *litchis*" I said.

"It is none of your business. Take out your identity cards."

"Ram Singh, collect their identity cards" he ordered.

"And I would like to see you guys tomorrow morning at eight sharp at the Clock Tower Police Station." he said and moved out.

"Sir, please listen to us."

"Sir, we won't do that again but please don't take our ID cards."

"Please understand Sir. We won't repeat it."

We tried our best but they went off.

"What the hell did you guys do?", "Why were they here?" asked everyone to the three of us.

I was explaining the scene to them.

After a few minutes we heard the police siren. We sensed it was approaching us. The Doppler's effect was observed practically. The pitch of the siren kept on increasing. The police van stopped right in front of our room. DC and Ntini went out to talk to the cops on the matter.

"Don't interfere with us and send those three bastards out." said the cop.

DC and Nitin failed to convince them our innocence.

"Either you send them or we will arrest all of you." the cop said angrily.

We went out, the rest followed us to check out the matter. Cops were asking for the arrest of three of us for interrogation.

We pleaded for mercy but the cops were adamant. We were arrested, and charged for stealing litchis.

Also, we were asked to remain silent and follow their orders, or else a charge for disorderly conduct would be levelled against us.

Aditya, Manpreet and I had to surrender to the police for plucking *litchis*! Ya, to me it was strange. I was wondering about the police force who kill their time like this. Going to jail and getting interrogated for plucking a few litchis from the roadside seemed to be weird.

"Sit in the van without wasting any time." one of them shouted.

Aditya and Manpreet were tense and so was I. We had no option but to obey them. Aditya started weeping.

"Sir, we are innocent. Please forgive us." I requested them, knowing that it would not work.

We were forced to sit in the van. They took us away. I can still recall the faces of all my friends who were standing at the gate, helpless. We were taken to the Clock Tower Police Station. The interiors of the Police Station were much like the ones depicted in the movies. It had a wooden table in the center where another cop was sitting. To his right was a cabin, maybe for some senior officials. On our right were the lockups.

It was fifteen minutes past three in the clock.

"Were they going to hit us? What when my friends and colleagues would get information on this? What action would the college take against us? What if they called home and tell about it?" The thoughts bothered me. Neha, then I could declare that there was nothing bad left that I didn't face during my college days. What wonderful experiences college life was giving me. It was hard to imagine, but ya, I was going to jail.

The policemen dragged us into the lockup and asked us to remain standing.

The song '*Papa kehte hain bada naam karega, beta hamara aisa kaam karega*' ran in my mind when I was stepping into the lockup gate.

"Sir, here are the guys." said the inspector who brought us to his senior officer.

"Good to see them."

"Rajender pour hot water on them, I am coming." he directed.

Manpreet couldn't control his tears them. I was still keeping my cool. I was uttering something or the other continuously to the inspector. I was trying to convince him.

The senior inspector entered the lockup with a belt in his hand.

"*Aaj ye mujra karayega.*" said Aditya.

"Sir, we are engineering students. We belong to good families. Are you going to beat us for plucking *litchis*?" I tried.

"Don't try to be innocent my boy." he said pulling my cheeks.

"Rajender, get Sarita here" he shouted.

Inspector Rajendar, brought a girl who was badly bruised. She had blue spots on her face, seemed as if somebody had beaten her brutally. She was wearing a *salwar-kameej*, her *dupatta* was torn. She looked terrible.

Within a minute I understood the matter. The police was going to charge us with rape. I looked at Manpreet and Aditya and found that even they realized what the police was going to do. But how were we going to prove ourselves innocent?

"Identify." asked the officer to the girl who was supposedly the victim.

She came close to us. Her condition was really heart breaking. I was taken aback to see the way she had been beaten. She was not able to speak because of her to swollen lips. She was watching each of us carefully. She came towards me and looked at me from head to toe. There was no expression on her face. She kept on watching me blankly.

She passed on directly to Aditya passing Manpreet. I guess she passed him because she must not have noticed any sikh guy away the culprits. She went close to Aditya, and paused!

Before anyone could realise something Aditya burst out in tears. "Sir, there is some confusion." murmured Aditya. He was extremely-frightened.

The officer stared at Aditya and then took the girl out. We remained standing motionless. I felt that our brains had stopped working. We were not able to understand what was happening to us.

The officer returned in a few minutes. His actions had changed. He walked differently. I could see the anger in his eyes. Before entering the lockup, he pulled out his leather belt and smashed it hard on the iron railings of the lockup.

All three of us started pleading with him. We were so frightened that even at the loudest, our voice was not audible. It sounded just like a whisper. "*sadak pe itni raat kya kar rahe the tum log? beh.........*" shouted the officer.

"Sir, we had just gone for a walk." said Manpreet.

"And when we were returning to our room, we saw some *litchis* hanging to the street. So, just thought of eating some and taking a few for our friends." I tried to explain.

"*Tujhse poocha maine? Tu hai kya Sardar?*" he shouted again and smashed his belt on the floor.

"No Sir, I am not a sikh. He is a sikh." I pointed out to Manpreet.

I was actually confused as to why the officer thought that I was a sikh was finding me the Sardar, when Manpreet was standing there. He was even wearing a turban, so why could the officer not identify him. Is this the way they are trained to be in the Police Force?

"No No Sir, I am not a Sardar." Manpreet shivered.

I was puzzled.

The very next moment I realized that I had made a blunder. The officer was asking him who the head of the group was . Sometimes when you are trapped badly in some situation then your mind stops working. But it happened with me for the first time in my life, otherwise I have a very witty mind.

"Are you finding it a joke?" the officer shouted in irritation.

"I am sorry Sir. I am sorry about it."

"You guys are lucky that Sarita has not identified you." said the officer.

His words gave a feeling of great delight. "Thank you sir, now can we just leave?" hurriedly I asked.

"Not so easily my dear. *Abhi to tumhe kai tamashe dikhane hain. Saalo raat ko sadko pe ghoomte ho*" he shouted.

"Sir, please Sir" said Manpreet.

"Ya, you may leave".

. It seemed as if we were waiting for this order since time immemorial. We felt like we have won the world. All three of us Manpreet, Aditya and me hurried to get out of the lockup.

"Where are you going Sweetie?" the officer put his hand on Aditya's shoulder.

We all stopped.

"You guys move out" ordered he to me and Manpreet.

Aditya started shivering. A stream started flowing through his left thigh. It kept on making its way to his shoes. His trousers went all wet. A yellow patch formed along his feet. The size of the patch kept on increasing. He was not able to speak a word. He was badly terrorized.

"What the fuck is that?" asked the officer.

Aditya fainted.

"Sir, please allow us to go" pleaded me.

"We are not the ones you are searching for. Please let us go" cried Manpreet.

He didn't bother to listen to us. He called Rajendar to attend Aditya and asked him to get Aditya back to his senses. We kept on pleading.

It rose 4:30 in the clock. I and Manpreet were standing outside the lockup helpless. Aditya was lying inside and an assistant was spurring water on him. Another cop entered the station with three guys handcuffed. "Sir, they are the ones who raped."

It gave us a sigh of relief. I to myself, thanked the cop who brought the real culprits. It was now the time to leave, I thought. By that time Aditya also got back to his senses.

"Sir, they work for *Litchi Gang*" he pointed us, "We are fed up with the daily complaints from the residents of Kalidas Road" he added.

Another ditch was created for us. The feeling of relief lasted not even for a second. "Litchi Gang!!" I and Manpreet exclaimed. "Sir, what the hell is this Litchi Gang now?" I asked in frustration.

"Please leave us, we have our external exam tomorrow" Manpreet pleaded.

"They are professionals Sir. The chief is from Jaipur, the masterminds in their gang are from Delhi and Haldwani" reported the policewala to the inspector.

He gave a terrifying look to all three of us. "Get back into the lockup" he shouted.

"Sir, please listen to us" Manpreet said.

"Shut up. Tell me which all places do you supply the litchis?" asked the inspector.

"Sir, we are students in DIT" I replied.

"Did I ask you? *Tu hai na sardar tere gang ka. Teri to dhang se leta hu*"

While the conversation between the police and three of us was going on, DC and Nitin managed to call the SP Office, Dehradun City. They explained the whole story and requested for our leave. At around 4:45 am the landline phone lying on the table of the Inspector rang.

Yes sir. Yes Sir the inspector said and hung up.

He came near to us and said "I'll leave you guys on one condition."

"We are ready for any of your conditions but please leave us Sir." cried Aditya, breathing heavily, his nostrils dilating.

"You have to be punished." he said.

"We are ready for any punishment Sir." I said.

"Get into the van then." he ordered. "No Sir. No Sir. Sir Please" cried Manpreet.

Putting us into the van must have made Manpreet to think of fake encounters. We were all very frightened. But we got into the police van. The inspector sat in front, next to the driver and ordered him to drive us to the Clock Tower.

The Clock Tower is located at the beginning of the Rajpur Road in Dehradun. It is a 78 feet tall tower built by Englishmen in early nineteenth century. When the Police Van was heading for the Clock Tower, I thought that the Police is going to shoot us and some kinda

Shaheed Smarak will be added to the surroundings of the tower. "Avi, what is he up to?" asked Manpreet pointing at the Inspector sitting on the front seat.

"Listen." I pulled Manpreet and Aditya close to me and whispered, "I have an idea."

But Manpreet intervened, "Please Avi, not again. It was because of your plan that we have got into this near."

"Because of me?"

"Yes. It was all because of you." Aditya supported Manpreet.

I was taken aback at their reaction, but decided to be positive, the situation demanded unity.

"Okay, I agree that it was all my fault. But please listen to me." I said.

"Why? You want us to get into more trouble?" Aditya asked.

"Maybe we get into more trouble.Do have you got some option?" I asked.

Both Manpreet and Aditya remained silent.

"What are you guys talking about?" asked the Inspector.

"Sir, Aditya is asthmatic. Please take us to a chemist's shop first" I said, don't know how and why. Aditya and Manpreet were surprised and looked at me. I myself didn't know what I was doing. Things were happening by themselves.

The inspector nodded at my request and ordered the van to stop at a medical store. "Go get the medicine quickly".

Aditya and I moved out to the shop and bought an inhaler spray. "Aditya continue acting like an asthmatic patient. Maybe it touches his heart." I whispered into Aditya's ear. We returned to the van.

We reached the Clock Tower.

"Come out." shouted the Inspector.

We stepped down and stood in a line. "Sir, please forgive us. We won't ever think of stepping out at night again" I said.

"Sir, its five clock. Please let us go. We have our paper tomorrow."
Manpreet filed the plea.

"Ya I will let you go but first turn around." he replied.

TURN AROUND!! We were shocked to hear that. Turning around meant that he was going to shoot us and frame a story in the next day headlines, "the police shot three gangsters who were trying to escape from police custody". "Oh no! No...." Aditya closed his eyes and turned around. Manpreet stood numb. My eyes went wet. My parents, my siblings, my relatives, Lisha I remembered everyone. I could see all of their reactions to the next day headlines. Was this going to be the end of my life?

"Don't you hear me? You f...... Turn around" the inspector shouted. We turned opposite. The song m*era rang de basanti chola* from the movie The Legend Of Bhagat Singh got played in my imaginations.

"*Distance rakho beech mei*" the inspector shouted again, which made us stand apart from each other. Aditya fainted, the second time.

"Aditya...." I and Manpreet screamed and ran towards him. The inspector also came to check out. Aditya didn't respond. I pulled the spray out of his pocket and sprayed into his mouth. "Uhuu Uhuu....." irritatingly he coughed. And his expressions conveyed me that he was acting deep into the character of an asthmatic patient.

Hats-off to his acting in such a crucial situation.

"Leave him you two. He will be okay" said the inspector. "I know that you guys are not the ones we are looking for. But you have made a mistake for which I need to give you punishment, so that you don't repeat it in future." he said.

Manpreet and I nodded.

He ordered us to do sit-ups until he finishes his tea. "*yahi pe?*" I asked, as we were standing in the middle of the road. There was hardly any traffic except some auto-rickshaw walas. "*To kya Ambedkar Stadium le chalu tujhe?*" he shouted.

Quickly we started with the sit-ups. Though Aditya stood up, he was saved from the humiliation. The inspector had mercy on him. I was feeling embarrassed to do sit-ups in front of the auto-rickshaw walas but there was no option. But it was definitely much much much better than a third degree in the lockup. "Catch hold of your ears." the inspector shouted again.

"Can't he have his tea in peace?" I whispered in Manpreet's ear.

"Shut up and keep doing the sit-ups." Manpreet replied back in whisper.

Manpreet and I did around fifty sit-ups but the bloody tea in the cup wasn't finished. When we were around the eightieth sit-up, the inspector asked us to stop. We were panting badly. "Sorry sir, we would never come out of our room at night." I apologized.

"You must take care of that. You know yesterday a girl was raped there at Kalidas Road, what if you guys were caught on that spot? Anything wrong could have happened. So be careful." he said, more politely.

"Yes Sir." we said in chorus.

"Now leave and prepare for your paper." he ordered.

"Yes sir, sorry sir." we said and walked away briskly.

Let's rule the world

" *Avi, ek baar fir se batao na Litchi churane waala kissa.....please*" Lisha said to me on phone, laughing heartily.

"Shut up Lisha. What's there to laugh?"

"Oh god....why does it happens with you always! Waise I would have loved *agar tumhe dande padte*"

"You know what...." I said interrupting her.

"What?" she asked, still laughing.

"Stop laughing first." I ordered.

"Okay, I'll try to. Tell me what you were saying."

"Lisha I have decided to try for a career in Civil Services. I want to be an IAS" I said.

Lisha could not believe her ears. "The guy who cannot read newspapers properly is thinking of IAS. Avi, have you even read your course books? And please don't forget that you failed in social studies three times." she said.

"I know that. But I have decided and I am soon going to join a coaching class for preparations. And then nobody would dare to touch me for plucking litchis" I said.

"Is that the reason you are planning for IAS?" she asked, laughing like anything.

"Shut up dumbo. Please listen to me seriously"

We talked about it for two hours on the phone, discussed the career and scope, the feasibility of joining a coaching class, and finally she supported me and appreciated my decision.

I started preparing for civil services examination. To give momentum to my preparations, I joined regular coaching at IAS Academy in Race Course, Dehradun.

When we go through the preparation process for civil services, we find ourselves a wiser person. We actually come to know about many things which we are not aware of. Constitution, history, geography, physics, chemistry, law, mathematics, economics, biology, current affairs, public administration were a few subjects amongst the complete list which needed to be read thoroughly to combat the level of this exam.

When I started preparing for the Civil Services examination I realized the core problem with the people of our country. We keep on arguing without even knowing about the details regarding the issue. People hate Gandhi, Nehru, people hate Hitler even I used to. But when I read about them, my views completely changed. Don't you think Neha that we are still more reflexive to the things which we hear rather then the concrete evidences.

People oppose Nuke deal, people talk about India's relations with other countries, people talk about increasing terrorism but people never talk about fool-proof solutions to these problems. Building castles in air by sitting within the four walls of house, is far different from facing the core realities at national interest.

I personally feel that the curriculum-content of civil-services must be injected into each level of education. Every child born in India must become aware of the grass roots problems of the society.

In its real sense IAS preparation not only imparts huge lumps of knowledge but builds up confidence, public speaking skills, logical reasoning, positive attitude, analytical views, etc. It helped me a lot.

Though I was pursuing engineering, I chose civil service as my career to utilize fully my technological concepts in managing the civil administration and help the nation in improving its bureaucracy. Bureaucracy is the steel frame of our country and must be a force to reckon with.

That was the reason I opted for it. I find it to be one of the best decisions of my life. In fact, it became the turning point in my life. I stepped in third year, the fifth semester of engineering. Engineering has been very difficult for me. I can't tell you how I managed to clear my papers.

When I was in first year, I faced a hell of a lot of difficulties in cramming the bullshit of Mechanical engineering. Thermodynamics, Strength of Materials, the equations for beams, trusses, the energy flow equations used to give me heebie-jeebies. Day and night I spent in cramming them. My friends used to make fun of me. They used to say that I was in love with thermodynamics as I used to murmur the equations throughout the day. I didn't sleep at night. I used to write the equations again and again. Some of the freaky ones even said that I used to masturbate with RS Khurmi in one hand.

I used to ignore such comments as I had to pass the paper anyhow. I didn't leave any stone unturned, and it helped me to clear the papers with a good percentage.

I entered the second year. The subjects became tougher. My academic standard deteriorated. I wondered the game of zeroes and ones. Every subject in our stream had zeroes and ones as its base. I regretted my decision of choosing Electronics & Communication as my specialization.

I never thought of playing with Zeroes and Ones in all the subjects in curriculum. Sometimes I felt like eliminating all zeroes and ones from this world. Why the hell can't the electronics jump to number 2! Zero one zero one….. ahhhhhhh!!!!!!

Well, by this time Ria became a very good friend. She used to help me out in my studies. I remember the classes she took of me in Central Library, on the terrace, in the cafeteria where she used to give her best in making me understand something and where I always kept on talking about all the things other than studies. I used to ask her about Lisha. I used to take her help in climbing the stairs of love for Lisha. I used to ask her about the emotions of the girls. I used to ask her about the gifts to be given and everything that I wanted to know regarding Lisha's matter.

Many a times she got annoyed at the way in which I studied. But like a most beautiful understanding partner she used to accept all my insincerity. And to my surprise, from that time she became my teacher and guide for each and every subject and till the end of my engineering, I was totally on her during my exams. Without her I couldn't imagine myself appearing for papers. Ria understood my psychology well and helped me greatly in preparing for the internal as well as external exams.

"When the A/D converter inverts the output, a signal bit is sent by the transponder to the communication network……" Ria was explaining.

"Ria you know what, Arvind Sir was asking about me, for organizing the cultural night." I interrupted.

"We will talk about this later Avi. Please concentrate." she requested.

"So, when the signal bit is sent to the communication network, the polarity of the diode gets reversed."

"Which cream have you applied Ria? I can smell Nivea." I again interrupted.

"Go to hell Avi. Why are you not studying? I have come long the way through to make you understand this and you are least bothered." annoyed she said.

"Okay Okay let us get back to studies. *Par ye batao aaj tum itni achhi kyu lag rahi ho?*"

She pulled my hair. And burst out in anger.

"Sorry sorry dear. I won't disturb you now. Please proceed."

This was the way our classes proceeded. Actually I didn't take interest in the subjects due to lack of practicality in understanding. Imagine you are reading about radars, antennas, fibre optics, microwaves, etc and you have never ever seen their functioning practically. So, gradually I lost my interest.

And that may be the reason that made me think of the Civil Services.

It was 25 September 2004 when I first attended the free counseling session at IAS Academy by Dr. A.R Rawat. It became a turning point in my life. The two hours session went off like two minutes. The way of presentation, the content in his speech highly attracted me. He is a great motivator. That two hour session laid a great impact on me. His influence was unlimited.

"IAS is the post wherein you hold the power to decide the future of the people, the society and the nation as a whole" sir said and started the counseling. He showed me the core realities of this service. He made me see the life of a civil servant beyond the red light brand.

On 29th September I joined the academy. I was put into the special batch on weekends as the other five days I had college. I packed up my bag and went off for the first class to my ultimate dream in life. While in my way to the academy I called up Lisha "Hi! Lisha; I am going for coaching" I exclaimed in pride.

"That's great Avi. Wish you all the good luck. But your classes have bought my time" sweetly she said.

"Will catch you after the class. You will be given your time dear." I said and hung up.

I reached the institute, parked my bike and climbed up the stairs for the classroom. I sat in the second row as the first was already occupied by the students who were regular in class. And at 3:15 sharp the lecture started. Sir began with Modern Indian History. The great battle for independence of 1857 was the event, from which the lecture picked up fire. The way Rawat Sir was delivering the lecture mesmerized me. I could actually visualize the scene which must have happened during the revolt. The modulation in his voice gave splendid expressions to the narration. I was greatly impressed by the information content in the lecture.

After the class was over, I went into a mood of self-realization. I found the content of my knowledge low. It was humiliating. The class had opened my eyes. I decided to work harder on my knowledge base. I pledged to work day and night to increase it as after all Knowledge is Power. I took my cell phone out to look for the missed calls and messages as during the class I hadn't get a single second to think about it. I found 126 missed calls. All of them were Lisha's!

I was about to call her up when my cell buzzed. It was Lisha. "Sweetie how was the class? I was missing you." she asked in a very excited way.

"Ya it was great! But I am not in a good mood. Talk to you later."

"Why what happened? Wasn't it a nice experience? Weren't there any hot chicks?" she asked.

"*Nai Lisha wo baat nai hai.* Class was awesome. But you know it made me realize that I stand nowhere when it comes to knowledge" I said.

"Oh ho......*itni si baat pe mood saddy saddy! Cummon Avi, ab aise mood off karne se to knowledge nai aayegi na. Kal ham saath baith ke discuss karenge aur schedule bhi banayenge.* Now smile please"

I was silent. "Achha bba close your eyes." she said.

I was still silent. "mmmmmmuuaahhhh". She kissed me on the phone. I smiled "Lisha, you are too much."

"And you are *magarmuch* my sweetie." I returned back to room lost in my own thoughts.

I prepared a time table for my IAS studies. I asked the hawker to get me the five recommended monthly magazines and government journals regularly. I started reading newspapers. I read stuff that interested me, bored me, baffled me, and dozed off in my seat. I read stuff that pricked up a noble thought, a philosophy that appealed, I gazed at pictures of old temples and ruin, new buildings, battleships, and monuments. I read about the formation of mountains, the origin of earth, about science, about literature, almost about everything.

The lack of knowledge created an interest in book reading. I made a habit to read one book every week, which was out of my curriculum. I learned much from the books. I remember how I was equipping my mind all the time. I read a certain amount of good stuff. Those days were very busy for me. I got up everyday at seven, and did not get to bed till three at night. I practised my schemes of study. There were still many dark corners in my mind.

One day after going from college I got stuck with some pending work of the IAS tuition. The whole night I kept on making notes of our Constitution. I didn't bother to see the clock till Aditya got up to get ready for college. Aditya was surprised to see me studying till morning and so was I. After having had breakfast I slept. I woke up in the evening when my phone beeped. I reached for it sleepily, hold it up and read, "*tum mehnat kar rahe ho achhi baat hai par that doesn't mean........ok leave it*". My instant reaction was to call her.

She didn't receive my call. I messaged her "Sorry dear. Please talk."

She called me back at night. "Hi…..where were you Lisha. I was so tensed!" I said.

"Friends had come to the room." So, didn't get time to check out the phone. Sorry" she said rudely. I couldn't understand why she was reacting this way.

"Friends! Lisha, are you trying to say that your friends are more important than me?"

"Of course not but yes the purpose for which they came was important"

"Will you please tell me directly?" I requested.

"Nothing Avi, they had just come to celebrate my birthday."

An unusual silence fell I was not able to take what I had just heard from Lisha. How could I forget that? That was a heinous deed. "Lisha I am so sorry. Please listen, I am feeling bad from the bottom of my heart. Lisha we are going to Rajaji Park tomorrow" I said.

"No Avi. Please don't be so kind. And by the way I have classes tomorrow and no out-pass."

"I don't know. You are in final year, don't tell me that you have to attend classes! And I know that you can arrange the out-pass. Stop making excuses na. Dear I love you and want to give you a surprise. Please don't deny." I urged.

"Okay but......but you have to pick me up from the college gate itself. And that doesn't mean that I have forgiven you." she said.

I always felt that I was too good for the task. I could *patao* her easily.

"Okay okay don't forgive me but please be ready on time tomorrow. *Banda haazir ho jayega theek dus baje.*" I said.

We missed our lectures next day and went to Rajaji Park. It is a national park and very famous for its elephants. We didn't go into the main park. There was a huge lawn adjoining the park. I parked my bike at some distance and we made ourselves comfortable on a bench, which was greatly covered by bushes at the back.

"Why have you chosen this seat? It's the odd one out." she enquired.

I gave a naughty smile. "Shut up you cheapster" she said, with a *kaatil* expression.

I went pink, couldn't help it. "What did I do?" I said, trying to appear cool.

"I know....whatever gets done is my deed no?" she mentioned, perfect girlish *nakhre.*

The whole world on one side and her *nakhre* on the other. I guess that the gravity of the other would be more. I loved her *nakhre*.

And that made me give a naughty smile again. I couldn't help it. "Will you please stop looking at me" she said, feeling self-conscious.

"Hey Sweetie, I got you a present." I said.

She moved close, excited. "Really?". She laughed, almost as if she couldn't believe it herself.

"Really." I said.

"You didn't remember my date of birth! How did you remember to get a gift for me?"

"That was the surprise I was talking about. Now please close your eyes." I said and pulled the small packed box out of the pocket and handled it to her. "Look!"

She opened her eyes slowly, and shouted in excitement "Wow, that's so lovely."

Her pitch startled me; I slipped from the bench, and landed on the ground. It was hard, rugged and uneven. Pointed stones pinched my bums. "Ouch!".

"You are a real joker." she said and helped me to get up.

"It made me think of you and me." I said, pointing the gift. The gift was a moving show-piece of a passionately kissing couple.

"Avi, you are too much." she said.

"You liked it?"

She kissed me hard on my cheek, "This much!"

"Avi, you remember when we first spoke to each other?"

"I remember everything you've ever said to me." I said, looking steadily into her eyes. I pulled her a little closer and buried her nose into my shoulder. Her breath against my chest was destroying my ability to understand anything else.

I leaned in to murmur into her hair, my voice all deep, "Lisha, I am going for an expedition next week."

"Expedition! And what do you mean you are going? What about me?"

"No, actually sir is taking us for an educational expedition." I said, in a lower voice.

"Ask him about me. I would also like to go"

"No Lisha….actually, only the girls from our coaching class can join," "Sir won't allow anyone else" I said, sounding helpless.

"Okay……For how many days?" she asked, very tense.

"For a week. But only if you permit." I said.

One thing I would say that her tear glands were always active. She was very sensitive. Even a thought of me getting away would take her breath away. And tears start flowing down her cheeks.

"Arrey…kya hua? I am not going, I just asked you." I said, holding her tight in my arms.

"No…no you go. But I'll miss you."

I didn't quite know what to say. I just sat there looking at her, at a loss for words.

The Chineese
attack

We opened the geographical map of India. There were several places where we could plan to go on our tour. On a general consensus we planned a tour to Laddakh. At eight in the evening we decided that Laddakh was the right choice for our first adventure tour.

We were given a precautionary lecture by Rawat Sir. We were told about High Altitude Sickness, about the acclimatization, about the bad weather conditions and about all the preventive measures to be taken. We were asked to carry torches, a first aid kit, grocery, chocolates and bags full of woollen clothing.

"So, boys and girls be on time tomorrow" he said and allowed us to disperse.

I can say that one of my dreams – an expedition across the Himalayas – was about to be realized. We had planned to go above 14000 feets in mountains. Our route included the crossing of six high passes, including two of the highest motorable passes in the world: Khardung La and Tanglang La. The expedition was not only going uphill to the passes but also a journey along the beautiful valleys and contact with other culture. From that moment India surprised us every day in many situations. We didn't know that then, but it was to be like that until the end of the expedition.

I equipped myself for the trip. I got the clothes and the other things ready. The desire to reach Laddakh was uppermost in me. Sumit and I reached the meeting place before the scheduled time. After all, the excitement was continuously thrilling us! We waited for others to arrive, it took more than an hour for all to come. All came but one girl.

"We will pick, Tia up from her place." sir said. We got into the car and we moved for picking her up from her place. Sometimes I feel that I should have been a girl, I would have loved to enjoy such privileges.

We just wished the girl to be cute, else the trip would be a total shit. We were waiting at the main road outside her house. Ten minutes later, we saw her coming.

"Jackpot" Sumit said in excitement.

Akash's mouth remained open. I thanked god for listening to my wish. The girl was really pretty. She wore a blue track suit on which *Singapore Convention'02* was printed. "She has definitely been to Singapore." I said to Sumit.

"We will have a great time dude." he clapped his palm onto mine.

Our team had nine members. Let me introduce all of them. The team was headed by Dr. A.R Rawat, teacher in the coaching class and an experienced mountaineer. He is a pro at of trekking expeditions. No knotty problem was too difficult for him, Mrs. Rawat, Rawat Sir's wife, Jaggi, an old aspirant of civil services and student of sir, stays in Delhi, Vishal, friend of Jaggi, Shikha, came in coaching, Tia, earlier an IAS aspirant now in Indian Defence Forces and was the most beautiful girl in the coaching class, me, Sumit, my friend from DIT and Driver, Jaggi hired from Delhi.

Jaggi looked like an old-fashioned *aashiq* type guy, who seemed to have joined the trip just for Tia. And his friend Vishal appeared to be a boring person. It seemed like he has never seen the world outside books. Shikha was always mute. She remained as silent as the instant after a big explosion. Sumit was as entertaining as ever, he remained on his phone till we crossed the local network, always busy with his girl friend. It seemed like he made his girlfriend count the number of breaths he took. Not a single second free.....huh!! I was happy that my situation was not like her.

So the team of nine departed from Dehradun to Manali the next day. Jaggi and Vishal were sitting next to the Driver on the front seat. Sir, Ma'am and Shikha were in the middle one and Akash, Sumit, Tia and I were on the back seats. Sumit and I were sitting together and Akash adjusted himself beside Tia, Tia facing Sumit and Akash facing me. I was missing Lisha, I missed her badly. I wished she was with me on the trip.

Sumit and I didn't know anyone in the group, so we decided to entertain each other. We cracked some foolish jokes and laughed. We passed comments on the other team members, to kill time. We walked in silence for the first fifty kilometers, occasionally exchanging some very dull, languid jokes with others as well. Jaggi was busy testing his worst collection of songs. *Bullet* was rocking the journey!! Thanks to the music shops at our first destination Paonta Sahib, where I could get some good tracks. Tia and Sumit together appreciated me for that. That was the first time when we talked to each other. That was what I was looking for since the time we started with our journey. Well, the talks continued and we introduced ourselves to others one after the another.

After the short break at Paonta Sahib, we headed for Mandi.

After four hours of bumpy ride from Paonta Sahib we reached hotel Rising Star at Mandi. Sir booked two rooms, one for the boys and the other for girls, ma'am and sir himself. Lucky he! The rooms were pretty good and far better than what we had expected. Actually it was an economy tour and sir had already informed us about the non-five star facilities. He warned us of zero-comfort and no-luxury during the complete journey. But at this destination the rooms had all facilities, the most important hot water. After the quick brunch I had a long hot water bath. Sumit, Jaggi and Akash didn't bathed. We got out of our room by nine and found the others already waiting. Sir and Tia were busy making the documentary. Out of the main door of the Hotel I saw Tia describing the beauty of the climate and the historical facts about the place with cameraman Dr. A.R Rawat. Both of them acted as if they were from a NGO or Discovery Channel. We guys also participated in the shoot. Tia asked us various questions separately. After about ten minutes recording we got into the car with the same seats and headed for Manali.

We reached Manali by three in the afternoon. Then for an acclimatization trek we decided to climb to the Hadimba temple. Just like you would climb Dhanolti hill to get acclimatized to Mussoorie altitude....poor joke anyways Sir, Me, Sumit, Akash and Jaggi enjoyed a brisk climb. Ma'am, Shikha and Tia remained seated in the car.

The temple was beautifully made, the interiors depicting the *pahadi* culture. We returned in an hour as we had to cross the Rohtang Pass before the sunset. Rohtang Pass comes in the bypass route from Manali. When we were on that route we came across a beautiful resort, just about twenty kilometers from the Manali town. Sir did a fantastic photography job there. The resort was the one shown in *Jab We Met* starring Shahid Kapoor and Kareena Kapoor. But I realized it years later when I saw the movie. It was no less than beautiful Switzerland. I wonder why people move out to foreign lands when here in India we have far more beautiful places we can visit.

We reached the mighty and famous Rohtang Pass at around eight. By the time we reached the pass, it was almost dark. "I told you to be fast, now see it is pitch dark here" Sir said angrily to all of us. I was surprised as to why we were held responsible for that.

He was the one busy photographing! But none of us uttered a word.

The weather turned ugly it started snowing heavily. Visibility was almost nil. We couldn't think of getting back as there was no space to turn the car around. And after all it was just the beginning of adventure in the expedition. I was prepared for the worst. So, I enjoyed the ugliness of weather.

"Keep on driving. We will freeze deep into the snow if we stop. Keep moving." ordered Sir in a firm but tense voice.

Sir and Ma'am were doing some serious discussion, might be about the weather. Shikha was sleeping. Jaggi and Vishal were playing the role of navigators and Tia was lost in her thoughts.

"Has anyone seen this much snow before?" I asked in the belief that we must keep our cool else we always land up in a mess.

"Guys, isn't it like a Hollywood film?" I said to break the fearful silence.

"Avi, don't you see something serious here?" Akash agitated.

"Oh that means I should look scared and start weeping" I answered.

"Shut up you guys." Sumit asserted his presence.

"Come-on guys we are on an adventure trip. Don't forget that." I reminded.

If Lisha had been here, how romantic it would have been.......I was thinking.

It started snowing more heavily. The driver was finding it hard to drive. The turns were very sharp and the road became slippery. Very carefully he kept on driving. Finally we crossed the Pass in about two hours. You can imagine the difficulties we had faced crossing the seven-eight kilometers distance in two hours. But we didn't lose our patience. And father did the driver. He really had the guts to drive in such worse weather conditions. I respected him for that. It struck eleven by the time we were on the other side of the Rohtang Pass. There was no place to take shelter.

I had carried some coffee cans for any emergency during the journey, but these eventually became our dinner. There was no option but to stay in the car itself.

Early next morning, we began the survey of the mountain, which was at an altitude of about 12500 feet. The scene here was completely different from that on the other side: Manali. No vegetation was visible, all the land and the hills were completely covered with snow. I felt like skiing but was dying of hunger. To our surprise, after travelling thirty kilometers ahead we saw a *Dhaba*. Things moved fast thereafter. We hurriedly rushed into it. I took a cup of tea. The rest of the members of our learn were searching for washroom. I didn't. It was below freezing point, what would have I used to wash? Water had frozen. So, I didn't attempt to take the risk. Also, I was not feeling like, maybe because I hadn't eaten the previous night. And how could I have, when it was not available!

Well, in twenty minutes we flagged off from there. It was four-thirty in the clock.

The non-stop travel, excitement, newness, all finally pushed us into an exhausted sleep. After two hours I stirred sleepily awake. I looked around through gummy eyes and struggled up, wondering where I was. A feeling of total fear went through me as though each cell in my body had been touched with ice. I really didn't want to get up.

None of us on the back seat were feeling great. But I was trying to boost the moral of everyone, as we had gone on an adventure trip. Actually I was trying to impress the only beautiful girl in our team, Tia, because I desperately needed good company for the whole journey.

After the hectic night at Rohtang Pass, we felt more like dead men then living human beings. Akash's knee was in deep trouble, Sumit was feeling like vomiting. My head was on rock concrete. Tia, Ma'am and Shikha were getting into the High Altitude Sickness Zone effect. Tia had already picked up a few degrees on mercury.

She was not feeling well. I tried helping her as best as I could. When the car stopped for us to take medicines, I helped her to swing her feet on to the icy ground and push herself off the seat. Her feet began to vibrate as if she had Parkinson's disease.

She began to get up, in fits and starts. First her head, then her neck, then her bosom, and finally her stomach till she was sitting upright. "I am not feeling well Avi" she said and slept again. But I forcefully made her have the medicines. She had them in a semi-conscious state.

Outside it was early dusk, the snow was slipping into the twilight. A mist had started to shade the land gray, then a light snowfall swept in and blurred what little could be seen. It was all so different. I wondered what was happening in the plains now. We kept on moving to reach our next destination Chhatru, Chhatdu in Hindi. There was still an hour life to reach Chhatru when Tia woke up. She held my hand and said "Avi, I am feeling better now." Akash looked at me in an unusual way. I felt as if I had committed some mistake.

"Sir, Tia's fever is gone." I said happily.

"That's great. What about Sumit? Is he fine too?" Sir enquired.

"Yes sir, we are all having a great time." I replied enthusiastically.

The snowfall slowed down. It looked like heaven outside. Tiny snow-flakes were falling on the ground making it slippery. We had never seen snow before except in photographs where it lay like the skin of some dead white beast on the ground. I had not realized that it danced with such joy through the air, with beauty of a ballet dancer. Its touch upon us was hesitant as a child's.

Sir asked the driver to stop, so that he could take some photographs of the beautiful scene. We enjoyed the beauty of the location we were in. All of us boarded out of the car. We started playing with the snow. We made snow-balls and threw them at one another. And as Tia raced under each flake trying to catch it in her mouth, she could have sworn each one was alive as it playfully evaded her and settled on her hair or my woollen Adidas cap which she was wearing. One enterprising fellow made his way on to the back of her neck and rested there for quite a while.

Tia ran about, trying to swallow as many snowflakes as she could. It wasn't easy. Some bumped into her nose, others on her jaw, but it was exhilarating. She dashed about, her furry jacket flapping, sucking in the air so clean and clear that it felt like a miraculous new drink. She snapped at a flake, leaping up for it, and her teeth clicked on themselves. A flake fell on her eye and stung. She blinked trying to clear it and then brushed her sleeve over the eye.

It was beautiful watching her at that time. I was imagining Lisha doing that. I missed her a lot during the whole journey.

Jaggi and Sir were busy taking photographs every possible angle.

"Tia, come here", "Avi, Sumit and Akash you form a tilted queue behind her" said Sir.

"Is he shooting for the Oscar?" Sumit whispered in my ear. We assembled as per the orders.

After a couple of such poses, he said "Boys and girls please get inside. The weather is not good".

I couldn't understand what was bad in the weather. It was so romantic and wild at times. I would have created destiny if Lisha had been there. I planned to come back to the place with her and spend two-three weeks in the heavenly place.

Tia made a snowball and threw it at Sumit. Jaggi joined the game by throwing snow on Tia. Akash threw some snow back on Jaggi. And the game began. Vishal and Shikha stood aside and watched the crazy chaps silently. Even I enjoyed their play being the audience.

"Time to go Jaggi.…Tia" Sir made a call.

"Yes, we are coming" Tia said, and smashed a big snow-ball on Jaggi's face. It was so big that the whole of his face got covered with it. I went laughing. Vishal, Akash and Sumit joined me.

"We are getting late!" sir shouted.

Poor guys had to leave the snow-throwing game. We proceeded towards the car.

"You've never seen snow before, have you Tia?" gently I asked.

"I was born in Himalayas. I was an Eskimo!" she commented making a face as if I had committed some blunder.

"Oh! Okay Miss Universe", "Now let us get inside, sir has ordered." I reminded her.

We reached Chhatru at eight in the evening. There were some government quarters which were occupied by army most of the time. Luckily we got one room vacant. Sir had requested the army people for the rooms. He had demanded for two rooms but we were given one. The room was a very cozy one. The flooring, the walls and the ceiling were all wooden. There was a double bed with two bulky blankets, and a side table with three chairs. The toilet was attached at the other corner from the entrance. The size of the room must be around ten by ten feet.

"Arrey ye to shuru hone se pehle hee khatam ho gaya" I said, as soon as I stepped in.

Tia smiled. Jaggi gave a dirty look.

"We have to stay here till morning." sir said.

"But sir how can we? This bed can hardly accommodate four people." Tia said.

"That's true sir, it would be very difficult to adjust." Akash added.

I was surprised when he mentioned of *adjust*ing. Who the hell has asked him to share the bed and adjust. I wanted Tia to relax without any disturbances. I was getting possessive. I was showing extra care and was a little possessive about her because she looked and even talked like my cousin sister Eisha. Eisha is the cutest sister in the world. She is studying in eleventh standard right now. Pumpum is the name I like to call her from. She has grown a little fat nowadays so I have given her a new name "Great Khali", and I always make sure that whenever I call her from this name, she gets annoyed. I love playing pranks with her and she does the same. She is very naughty too. I remember one day, she offered me a glass of juice while I was on phone, talking to Sonal. I accepted it, unknowingly the trap which had been prepared for me.

That day I was wearing my Adidas lower, the black one and a red t-shirt. "Avi Bhayia, phone kab rakhoge?" she asked.

"Give me two more minutes" I requested.

She suddenly pulled down my lower. It went below my knees. I was helpless as I had the glass of juice in one hand and phone on the other. "Bye Sonal" I said and instantly disconnected the phone. Eisha was mad laughing. And to my surprise, I didn't scold her, instead I kept looking at her. She looked like a fairy in her original laughter. I pulled up my lower, tied the *naara* and then ran after her.

So, whenever I saw Tia, Eisha came to my mind. And no one in this world can see his sister suffering. So I lend my full care to her during the whole journey.

"I am dying to sleep" she announced and jumped onto the bed. Ma'am and Shikha joined her.

"Where are we going to sleep?" Sumit asked.

"Where there is a will there is a way" Sir answered, diplomatically.

"Sir, I am getting reminded of Darwin's theory of *Survival of the fittest*" I interrupted.

"Don't worry *ladke*, all of us will get adjusted" Jaggi said.

I wanted to retaliate. I wanted to knock him out. I didn't like any of his comment. But the time didn't demand that. I remained silent and gave a fake smile.

Sir, Sumit and, Jaggi sat on the chairs around the corner table. Ma'am, Tia and Shikha were already inside the blankets. I, Vishal and Akash sat on the corners of the bed. Driver made himself comfortable in the car. I guess he was the one who actually got proper space to rest.

"To kill the fever and cold fear, drink beer" Jaggi announced and invited everyone. I was least interested.

Sumit, Vishal asked for their pegs. "One-fourth with soda"
Vishal said. I had heard him for the first time in the whole trip. I
wondered that the guy who didn't say anything from Dehradun
to this place, loudly ordered his peg. "Might have been a great
boozer" I thought.

Jaggi served the pegs to all, starting from sir. Sumit, Akash, Vishal
picked up their glasses. Shikha demanded for a neat one, I was surprised!
Tia picked the glass which Jaggi announced that he had specially
prepared for her, I didn't like it at all.

Jaggi offered me too, but I refused "I don't drink".

"You can take in small amount, it will help in this weather" sir
suggested.

"No sir it is fine with me. And you just said that where there is a
will there is a way" I said and moved to the gate.

"Where are you going?" Jaggi enquired.

"I will be comfortable outside" I said.

I knew it had created a bad impression of my attitude but I never
like attending booze sessions. It depresses me, so I avoid it. I am not
against it but I don't support it in presence of girls and women even. It
is something against my ethics. I just wanted to disappear from the
scene and take Tia along with me. But Tia picked the glass, which
meant that I had to leave alone.

"Cheers" exclaimed everyone together banging their beer mugs.

My heart was crying. I could not see Tia having alcohol. I gave her a
disgusted look and moved out.

I stood by the pillar, lost in my own thoughts. I was disturbed. I
wanted to return back to Dehradun, to Lisha. All the romance and
adventure drained away. I took my mobile out and dialed Lisha's number.
But there was no network. I was exhausted. The fun journey had now
become a burden. I opened the picture gallery in my phone and scrolled
Lisha's photos.

After about fifteen minutes, when I was scrolling Lisha's album in my phone, Tia came. She tapped on my back "Hello….what are you doing here?"

"Oh hi…..well nothing. I was just searching for the network."

"Missing somebody?" she asked.

"Ya….missing everything." I said sarcastically.

Tia held my hand and looked into my eyes. "What?" I said.

"Let's go for a walk." she insisted.

"Your party host must be waiting for you." I said.

"I don't care."

"But he does. Go and get another peg for yourself" I said in mild irritation.

For a moment she stood still, and then she said "Avi, I didn't drink. I just took the glass in my hand to give company to all. I didn't know that you don't drink. When you refused, I felt so bad with myself. I wanted to come along with you at that moment only but that would have cropped fishy stories in Jaggi's mind, so I came late. I am sorry".

"Oh….I must say Sorry to you…..I took it the other way" I said, feeling bad of myself.

"It was none of your fault. Now give a smile" she said.

I smiled.

The clock showed 1:30 at night when we walked out. Heavy snowfall had left the ground fully covered with snow. A six-eight inch layer was formed all over. We were excited and tensed too.

Silently we moved away from the room. Both of us were tightly wrapped in the woolen stuff. I shared my overcoat with her. Her nose grew dark pink. Her lovely cheeks went red. She looked more like a polar panda. She actually looked wonderful.

It was dark outside. The distance only a feet ahead was translucently visible to us. Still we headed towards it. Heading down the way we passed away the army cottages, which were all silent like a calm sea shore. We loitered around the cottages. The wind which had been blowing since the evening had dropped and we were quite cosy in my overcoat. Tia breathed deeply and her already pink nose hurt with the clean coldness of the air. She exhaled watching her breath becoming smoke and then tried to blow smoke rings.

We enjoyed being together. We were telling each other about ourselves. "So do you have a girlfriend?" she asked.

I took out my cell phone and showed her the pictures of Lisha. "Is she your girlfriend? She is so pretty" she exclaimed.

"*Photography ka kamaal hai.*" I said and we both laughed together.

"Tell me about her, how did you fall in love with her? When did you propose her? When was your first date?"

I started answering to all her questions. I even disclosed some of the secrets which I have yet not told to anyone, Neha.

The night ended pretty soon after that. We returned to the cottage at around four in the morning.

The next morning, sir got the information about the blocked routes to Leh and Laddakh. "We are supposed to change our route, the routes to Leh and Laddakh will clear by next week" he said.

"Oh no.....we won't be able to go to Laddakh!" Sumit was disappointed.

"Sir, why not go to Chandrataal?" Jaggi said.

Sir agreed to it and conveyed to us complete information about the new destination, which was just 90 kms from this place.

"Let's rock Chandrataal." I exclaimed.

"Sir, Chandrataal was first visited by Aurangzeb na?" Tia asked.

"No, there is no concrete evidences as to who visited it first. Various fossils related to lives of people in different countries have been found there." he said, adding "Aurangzeb had once said about Chandrataal that 'If there is heaven on earth it is here'".

Sir is a mobile encyclopedia, I can say. You talk to him any topic you feel like and he will overload you with relevant information. We left Chhatru soon.

The road, I don't know why I am calling it a road, from Chhatru to Chandrataal was a track between the snow covered peaks and with the river Chandra flowing by its side throughout. I had always read that a river has flowing water. But this river changed my concepts, the water was frozen. It looked more beautiful than Antartica, an absolute dream.

After about fifty kilometers, we came across two-three stones which were dedicated to the people who had died there. At a place thirteen people from two cars were swept into the Chandra river in the course of a landslide. There was a small Durga Mata mandir made of wood, in remembrance to them. The wind was picking up speed and my head started to rock!

We reached Batal. It was the last stop before Chandrataal where we could get something to eat. We got off the car quickly and rushed into the only dhaba there. It had thecapacity of around thirty. We ordered nine teas. The first sip soothed my lips, tongue and the food pipe. The second sip seemed like normal tap water, tasteless. And the third sip went cold like an ice tea of Barista. The intense cold could now be seen through naked eyes.

We ordered for another nine cups. And then another nine. The chain of nine would have continued if the rate of teas had not been disclosed. Ten rupees per cup!

Well, sir made the payment and we sat in the car for the destination which Aurangzeb had immortalized! The route from Batal to Chandrataal was a trekking route. The road, again designating it wrong, was just eight feet wide, completely uneven. On one side was the hundreds of feet deep abyss and on then other side were frightening, snow-covered peaks. The driver was finding it difficult to drive the car, fully loaded. Everyone was shit scared when the driver was getting the vehicle out of the dangerous patches on the track.

We, the boys, stepped out of the car. On the turns, Sumit and I used to lean on one side of the car to give support. Killing strokes of chilled winds strike our face. My heart was sinking. We decided to walk and cover the route. Girls were lucky, they enjoyed the car ride.

Some of the turns were covered with snow. We had to clear it to make way for car to move. We carried on with our long walk to Chandrataal. Jaggi, the dude was having some trouble in breathing as well as a headache which made him walk slower than the usual. Sumit, Akash and I were trying to locate some shorter route, if any.

The first short-cut that we took almost saved two-three kilometers and we stopped at a point where I saw the route, though shorter, but sloping down. But what climbs down surely come up. My heart was sinking. But we took the risk of trying that path. At one of the snow covered rocks I bumped my ass because of a bounce and for a while thought my back was gone for ever.

Sumit and Akash helped me stand up. After a few yards we found ourselves stuck as a huge stone was lying right in the middle of the road. It was impossible to move, even by all three of us. We waited for the others to come.

In about thirty minutes, all approached the spot.

"God damn it" Shikha said.

I heard her speak for the first time in the whole journey. "Let us all push it towards the abyss." sir said. "*Driver ji aap bhi aa jao*" Jaggi said. We pushed it together in one go, and it rolled into the abyss to the river.

"All of you get inside the car. We are running behind time." Sir instructed.

We were all facing the high altitude problem. It was getting difficult to breath. I was panting like a dog, trying to breath. But I was managing my health quite well with the changing weather. Rest were all sick. Some had a headache, some vomitted, some had breathing problems, I was the only one in perfect form, staying on the back seat with Tia to see the frozen air and enjoying the beauty of the *Jab We Met* moments.

Akash was sitting with Sumit, away from Tia for the first time. I loved that.

After a few minutes the dead end of the road appeared. We stopped the car.

"Our destination is just a kilometer's walk from here" Sir said excited.

The sickness of everyone disappeared. We felt energized as if we had taken some energy pills. We formed groups of two and three and headed towards Chandrataal.

After ten minutes of breathless brisk walk, I realized that I had forgotten the banner in the car itself. The banner had a snow covered mountain as the back-drop and IAS Academy & All-Round Development Club written large font size in the front. It looked amazing. I wanted to get our pictures with the banner. To go back to the car, which was left 800 meters behind, was a foolish thought and to move ahead without banner was not to be thought of. Nobody else was ready to return to the car and get it.

I thus found myself in a dilemma.

I couldn't bear to move ahead without banner, but to return to the car was not to be thought of. Now that I had come along with it, I must get it, said the inner voice.

And I decided to return. "You guys carry on, I'll be back." I said and turned back.

"Wait, I am also coming." Tia stopped me.

"No, its okay. The car is far behind and you are not feeling well." I tried to stop her. But it was of no use.

We retraced our steps to the car, which was at some distance from where we stood. We walked along together, holding hands.

"So, how are you finding this place Tia?" I asked.

"Its heaven Avi!" she said, lifting her arms up and taking a round.

The place was in the foothills of upper Himalayas. On the other side of the ranges was Tibet and China. The Indo-Tibetian Border

Police guards the borders of this area. Spiti and Lahaul Valley region originate from these ranges. The mountains of these ranges are always snow-covered. And from November to late February, the whole valley remains inaccessible due to heavy snowfall.

Well, we reached the car. We unloaded the luggage from the back seat and pulled out the banner.

"Lisha would you like to have coffee?" I asked.

"Lisha!! I am Tia"

I shook my head. "Oops....Sorry....Actually I was missing her."

"Why didn't you get her along?"

"I thought sir won't allow" I said.

"Hmmm....so you are not enjoying the trip. I am boring you na." she said with a sulking face.

"I would have cancelled my plan if you were not part of the trip." I said.

Tia raised her brow "Achha?"

I nodded.

"Now carry these cans. I'll hold the banner." I said and we walked back. We walked slowly, we were facing difficulties in breathing.

"Sumit....Sumit" I shouted from a distance, when he was visible. The Chandrataàl could now be seen. We then moved faster. It was a beautiful lake with sky-blue colored water. It's beauty was glorified by the reflections of the snow on the peaks surrounding it. We reached the spot finally with the banner, dead tired.

Ma'am, Akash, Shikha and Vishal went for a walk to the lake, others kept sitting and enjoying the photography.

I wanted to sleep and relax for the rest of the day. Sumit kept telling me I was missing Lisha. And I kept telling him I was missing my breath more than Lisha. "If I can't breathe, I won't be able to miss my dear." I said.

The next hour passed in photography. The weather was getting worse with the ticking of the clock. So we moved back to the car, heading for Kunjam Pass.

After about ten minutes, Jaggi had nose bleeding for the first time. He was in really bad shape but we kept on moving as staying there could prove to be fatal. Tia felt a bit feverish. Akash was suffering from snow-blindness and Sumit had a bad care of sunburn. He was in great pain. The temperature had fallen suddenly.

We reached Kunjam Pass or Kunjam La as it was called locally. It was the deadliest. The sun had dawned by that time. And snow was still falling. The oxygen content in the air was lesser.

I think I am getting into the HAS zone, blood supply to the brain is getting weaker...... all nonsense thoughts were popping up in my mind. Jaggi's condition deteriorated. He was complaining of chest pain and breathlessness. He was not able to speak.

It was very difficult to tackle the situation at such low temperatures. His condition made us stop the car. He rushed out, I was trying to give him support but he fell on the road. He was shivering. His body had turned blue. Sir and Sumit came out of the car for help. The snow started directly hitting us on the face. My fingers were frozen and to keep them alive I kept banging them on to my thighs.

Sir, ordered me and Sumit to get Jaggi back into the car. He was in danger of having a heart attack! We quickly picked him up and rushed to the car. We made him sit with ma'am. She covered his ears tightly with a shawl, trying to keep the cold out. Everyone trembled in fear. I remember looking at each other with raised eyebrow and a scared grin. Sir ordered driver to drive the car at the maximum speed he could. He was not able to go above thirty as the road was very uneven and there were very sharp turns. On top of that, the low pressure at Kunjam La's high altitude was creating problems for the engine of the car to work efficiently. I guess the lack of oxygen was disturbing the combustion process. But we kept on moving.

Jaggi seemed to have stopped breathing.

"He is not breathing. He is not breathing" Ma'am said and fainted.

The situation went out of control. We tried not to tell the driver about of his death.

Time seemed to have frozen.

"Oh god!" Tia closed her eyes. Shikha was already unconscious.

I was not able to decide what to do, but somehow the whole thing gave me some momentum. I tried continuously to convey to the driver that everything was okay, nothing bad had happened. I was doing it so that he kept on driving safely.

Our condition worsened when the carrier on the car suddenly slipped to one side. We had to stop the car to put it back. I and Sumit jumped out and tried to catch hold of it. But we were not able to put it back as our hands shivered in severe cold.

We threw the rucksacks to the back seat where, Vishal, Tia, Akash were seated. It took us two minutes.

Sir, pulled Jaggi out and asked ma'am to help him. Ma'am was still not in her complete senses. Sir laid him on the road. And beat his chest. No movement was observed. I knew that we were already late.

"Does anyone know how to give mouth to mouth respiration?" The driver asked.

No...No...No and a number of No's were heard. "I will try." ma'am said and gave him the mouth to mouth treatment. No movement was seen. She slapped his face again and again. But there was no response. "Say something Jaggi" she cried on his chest.

"Ma'am, its severely cold. We must take him to the car, else all will get buried under snow." I shouted.

We got back into the car. Vishal was crying. The driver drove the car very fast to get some medical help. We all started praying to god for his life. "Oh god please help him..." Ma'am said, folding Jaggi in her arms.

A few minutes later, he breathed.

"Keep on patting him. *Driverji aap tez chalaiye, aage help mil jayegi.*" sir said, hurriedly.

After an hour we reached Losar, a small town at the opposite end of Kunjam La. By the time we reached there, Jaggi had started feeling normal. The other members couldn't get out from the shock. A severe migraine had already attacked ma'am, Shikha was unconscious, Tia vomited and shivered with cold, Sumit was fighting his burnt skin, and the rest of us were medically okay but physically dead tired.

I was so tired that my body had taken over and I wanted to sleep at the earliest. I was concerned about Tia. I lent my jacket to her and made her wear it, though forcefully. We took our shelter for that night with the dhaba people there.

"Avi, I hope you are feeling alright." Tia said. For the first time from Dehradun to Losar, somebody cared about my health.

"Ya dear I am fine." I replied with a sweet smile.

What more could I say? We all were still alive, gods must be crazy!

We returned to Doon safely. "What an amazing experience it was", I said to myself and smiled.

The to-be-Laddakh trip gave me a sweet friend forever.

Anything for you ma'am

The trip took seven full days. Lisha had remained tense each and every second of the clock for all the seven days. She used to try my number thousands of times a day, just to check out the availability of network, to hear me once. The next day in college, I met her.

"Hi sweetheart......I am back" I exclaimed.

"I am not talking to you." she said showing *nakhre*. The typical one.

"I know I know you missed me a lot. I missed you too." I said and hugged her.

"Leave me Avi. I am not interested in talking to you." she said, this time a bit irritatedly.

"*Achha theek hai nai batata tumhe Tia ke bare mei*" I said, tickling her jealousy bone.

"*Chup chaap se batao how the trip was.* Why didn't you call me once?"

"Yaar wo Tia ke chakkar mei time hee nai mila" I said, adding flavor to the J factor in her.

"Okay then go to hell with her". Perfect *nautanki*!!

"Arrey listen….". But she turned her face.

I knew what to say. I spoke out my heart. I told her how much I missed her. I cut the crap of teasing and told her how much I love her and her importance in my life. I promised her a date. I promised the evergreen Avi to her.

We decided to spend a day in Mussoorie.

It was 20th January 2005, I was ready at eight, having changed my dress a number of times, wore my new Levis jeans, pullover and the Adidas jacket and jelled my hair lavishly. I had shaved, showered, applied aftershave and then waited patiently.

I felt excitement spreading in my chest like a pleasant cactus.

I was patiently watching the chicks coming out of the college gate just to find her. The girls are in true sense the gamblers. They actually know the techniques to control us. After about forty minutes I saw her coming. She was nearly an hour late. I had seen almost all the students coming out of the college main gate, examined all the advertisements and banners hanging near the college gate many times.

I decided not to talk to her during the journey.

"Okay. Don't say anything. Sorry, I'm late, I know, I know," she said and sat down with a thump on the back seat of my bike.

I didn't say anything. I looked at her tiny nose. I wondered how it allowed in enough oxygen. Lisha was looking pretty. She wore black jeans with a red top and maroon jacket. She wore big ear-rings. I don't remember the color and design as I am allergic to jewellery. She put *kajal* in her eyes, which I was absolutely crazy about.

"What, say something," she said.

"I thought you told me to be quiet," I said.

She kissed me on the shoulder and said, "*achha baba ab galti maaf karo.*"

All my anger and resolution drained away within fractions of a second.

We started with our very first visit to Mussoorie. Yup! To Mussoorie on our very first one. We were extremely excited about it.

Lisha came and sat on the bike. In a typical heroic style, showing off our muscle power I kicked.

Something odd was definitely to be faced, *bhagwan chahta hee nai ke sab theek ho*. I mean it was really strange as to why it always happened to me. My friends and colleagues even asked me a why it was always me.

I kicked again but the bike didn't start.

I kicked again and again but it didn't. It seemed as if the engine was taking revenge for the time when I used to drag it without petrol. For the next half an hour I kept on kicking, tried my best to start it, but couldn't do it until some of my friends came and suggested to me to flick the key and start the ignition.

"Avi now that is something I could never have expected from you. You didn't even put the keys!" surprised Lisha.

Neha I was so lost in Lisha that........I believe you can understand why I forgot to put the keys. When you see a beautiful girl you actually forget everything. Even Einstein in his theory of relativity mentioned that "Time is relative. When you are with a beautiful girl, the whole day will pass like a few seconds. On the other hand when you are with a fat ugly lady, you will find a few seconds like years passing out."

"I just.....I don't know how it happened." I said and started the bike.

Though we were an hour late, we finally started off on our first date to Mussoorie.

We were out of the college area soon and Lisha began to take in the magnificence of the hillside. She was taken aback at how lovely it was. The sparkling trees, beautiful hills, the chilling foggy weather, all added to it.

Lisha was very frank with me and that was the thing in her which I loved most.

"I guess you are looking for some fun." she smiled. Her voice was low and husky. It felt as if a cat was rubbing itself against me.

"I am having a very good time," I sniggered nervously.

She sensed my nervousness and it was in her habit to take full advantage of my innocence. "You know Avi, the moment I saw you, I said, here's the guy who knows how to have a good time," her voice had traces of sincerity and mischief, which went under my skin and began to spread warmly. We kept on pulling each others legs and making fun of each other till we reached Mussoorie.

It seemed to be the coldest day Mussoorie had ever witnessed. We had plans to return by evening.

"Avi by what time will we be going back?"

"Oh darling, just don't worry. *Jahan ham hain wahan kya gam hain*! We will return before your hostel in-timings." I replied in an assuring voice.

I didn't even finish the sentence and it started raining heavily. We ran into a shop to protect ourselves from getting wet. But I thanked god for the changed weather as then I could spend a good romantic time with her.

You know sometimes god was so understanding! "Wow....isn't it like heaven?" she exclaimed.

"Ya, it is. *Aur heaven ki sabse sundar pari bhi mere saath hai*." I said.

"Haai........" she said, taking a deep breath.

The rain didn't stop till the evening. It grew more intense and it was impossible for us to even think of stepping down the hills by any conveyance possible. I had no option but to stay on in Mussoorie till the next morning.

At this exact point, as I was visualizing this, I felt a gun touch the back of my neck and a voice hiss "Move and you die". I was afraid of some hooligan but then I found Lisha playing a prank on me.

I didn't respond to the actuality of my senses as I was worried about the return journey. How am I going to manage? How will Lisha handle it? Where will we be staying?

Lisha came over. "Why are you so worried?" she asked, "*itna achha to ho raha hai mausam*" added.

I conveyed to her that we wouldn't be able to go back. "Lisha we need to find a place here in Mussoorie itself till the weather gets clear" I said.

Lisha got tense as now she had to make excuses to the Hostel Staff and even at home.

"Worry not dear. We will find good accommodation for ourselves" I said in sympathy, knowing that it would be very difficult to find a room as it was the peak season for tourists. It struck twelve when we found a room in a good hotel. We booked the room and went out for a walk.

A lot of questions were troubling our mind but we managed to cope. Then and there I realized that whenever Lisha and I were together, all tensions used to turn to fun. We believed blindly on each other.

We stepped out in the night, the wind seemed to have a colder thrust to it than usual. In the middle of the Mall road was an old fountain and a statue of Indira Gandhi that the government had put up to pay tribute to her contributions. Right in front of the statue was the wired trolley. The trolley took the tourists to the topmost point of the Mussorie hills, but due to bad weather that day, it was non-functional.

We were mesmerized by the beauty of that night. "How come we have never been here before?" she questioned herself.

She regretted that we had never come here - it was our first visit to the heaven like place.

We had hardly walked a hundred feet when I saw a soft white dandelion rest on her left cheek. I brushed it away and to her surprise it felt cold.

"Its snow!!!" she screamed in excitement.

We looked up and there were many of them floating gently downward. They looked like the little bosoms of a tree, but when we touched them they turned to water. Lisha was looking beautiful like a fairy queen under the snow shed.

"Avi hold my hand" she insisted. I took her arm. She looked incredibly amused. I put my hand around her waist and came much closer. We kept looking into each others eyes. It seemed like everything had stopped around us. I couldn't really make out what the scene was on the street, I was lost in the eternal beauty she carried. She closed her eyes slowly. Her lips touched mine.

"I love you Avi" she said.

I fell back flat, my heart pumping so loudly I was afraid I would have to hold it with both the hands to control it. I remember the night, I hugged her tightly in my arms and warmth began to flutter in my chest as though my sternum had crystallized into butterflies and were trying to fly away.

"Take my jacket and make yourself comfortable Lisha" I tried to show confidence. Even I have seen in many of the bollywood block busters that putting jacket on girls shoulders works well. We then walked towards the hotel as I was dying in cold. I kept my hand on her shoulder and held her possessively in my arms.

We reached to the hotel in which we booked our room at around 2 a.m. It was a single room with a sofa, a small dining table, on which were placed a flower-vase and steel coffee mugs. There was a music system built in one wall, and a TV too. There were flowery curtains in the windows, a red silk hand-printed carpet covering the floor, a double bed with spongy mattress and a fluffy silky quilt seemed like it the room was giving an invitation to the newly wed buds. I knew that I had to be either *Shahrukh* of DDLJ or *Govinda* of Hero No.1.

"Lisha please don't take it the other way but as there's only a one bed so I will make myself comfortable on the sofa" I tried.

"Avi I don't wanna miss a single moment of this beautiful night" softly she spoke.

I was absolutely confused as to what did she meant. Was she inviting me? I felt a new feeling dawning inside me. My career, my teams, my awards, my struggle all this became secondary. I hoped to transcend myself and discover my inner-self, the love within. I guess in my case everything was going dramatic.

"I don't want to sleep. You order coffee and cookies and we will talk till the morning" she said.

"You're sure?" I asked.

"Yes of course." She siggled. She, stood up and kissed me on my cheek to show me the intense trust she had in me.

I pored over the menu card which was neatly placed on the dining table and ordered eight Cappuchinos, two each after an interval of forty-five minutes and Chocolate truffle cookies.

I don't know how she sensed nervousness in my voice.

"I guess you are not feeling self comfortable" she enquired. "Okay let me make you feel relaxed. If you don't mind…." she added.

I was mute.

She switched on the dining lights and the music system. Inside the room the darkness spread and the air seemed to beat to the rhythm of the music. For a moment I stood absolutely still, my eyes straining, but I could see nothing except the music system. She came close, held my hand and offered to dance with me. I wasn't good at it. But in no case I could miss the romantic moment, so I just started without caring the way I was doing. I was merely moving without being in time with the music. My arms and legs never quite seemed to be where I wanted them to be at approximate the same time, and my head seemed to have been stuffed with cement, going by its refusal to move.

You know I am not that bad at making moves but I guess I was nervous and even feeling conscious. But I could scarcely believe it. What a good time I was having.

The whole night we kept on talking about each other. We shared all our best moments and the embarrassing ones too. We disclosed the way we started liking each other and how we fell in love. The feelings transported us into nostalgia, took us back to the good old days when we saw each other for the first time. Multiple images of those good old days thronged our mind. We remembered the terrace of the stepped building of our college which remained covered with trees. There was no one there to disturb, which helped us to spend time.

It had rained heavily at night; the glass on the window had frosted. The trees shivered in the cold wind. I found that one of my greatest pleasure was looking at her sleeping in my lap.

By nine in the morning, the rain had reduced to a slow snivel and the soothing sun had put in a cameo appearance before setting up through the hills.

The weather went all clear and we headed back towards Doon.

Exploring
Lisha....Lisha's room

The next two months, went by in a total whirl. I had three things to do everyday. One attending the college, obviously not for studies but for the co-curriculars. Convocations and farewell party of our seniors were the mega events, I was working upon. Second, I had coaching for Civil Services preparation in the evening. The classes were on from three-thirty in the afternoon to seven-thirty in evening. And lastly I had to take out time for maintaining my percentage in academics also.

The busy schedule gradually created gaps between us. I didn't have time for her, which any relationship demands the most. I had always been overly-busy either with studying for Civil Services examinations or with other projects I had taken up. I was focusing more on my career, forgetting everything else, forgetting memories of our outings together.

Sometimes I felt really bad at my behavior and my changed attitude towards her. I had started taking her for granted. I never wanted that, but it had happened.

It was 10th April, late in the evening I had been fast asleep for many hours, I think, when the phone rang. "Hello?" Lisha's deep voice came crisply on to the line.

"Hi." I said sleepily.

"Are you up?"

"Just about," I said, sitting up in bed and cuddling the phone to my ear irritatingly.

"Can you go onto the terrace?"

"I am resting, can you just tell me what is there on terrace?" I said.

"You go first. I'll tell you."

"I am not going. I am very tired." I said. I couldn't believe I had said that. I had talked so rudely to her.

"Its okay. Well Happy Birthday." she said and hanged off.

"Hello….hello" I said, thinking that the line was still on.

Early in the morning, the next day, I called her up. But her cell was switched off. She didn't switch it on for the whole day. I tried more than a hundred times but always found the same. "What the hell does she think of herself?" I said to myself. A few seconds later, I realized that I had starting thinking only of myself. Why was I pushing her away from my life?

I wanted her back. I wanted my Lisha back. I wanted all the gaps to be bridged. I wanted the old memories back. I messaged her for a meeting. But I didn't see her messages or calls after that night.

After about ten full days, my phone beeped with the message tone I had set especially for her. I looked down and saw a message flash, "Hi. How are you?"

I messaged back quickly "I am not fine. Where were you?"

"Thought of not disturbing a busy personality."

I instantly called her up. Distances reduce when we talk. This time she received my call.

"Lisha where were you? Tried you more than a hundred times every day. What's the matter? What has happened to you?" I asked all the questions which had piled up in my mind for the last few days.

"Avi, so much has happened since I saw you last, you're a real star!" she said in sarcastically.

"What has happened? What are you talking about?" I asked with mild irritation.

"Leave everything aside. Avi, I had planned a surprise for you on your birthday but I didn't know that you would be busy on that day as well. I know that was again my fault, as I didn't take an appointment."

"Lisha please stop it now. You know na that I was busy with the Convocation Ceremony and then the test series in the coaching and now the farewell." I tried to explain.

"You must be happy na......"

I didn't know how to answer. But I knew that one aggressive or negative answer of mine would have multiplied the misunderstandings manifold. So I remained polite. An awkward silence followed.

"Lisha we must meet" I insisted.

"For that Mr. Busy needs to have some time", though her words hurt me, what she said was true. I was engaged with the farewell party's preparation.

"Let's meet on 23rd. I will be waiting for you eagerly." I said.

"I will see."

I put down the phone slowly, saying nothing.

23rd April was a very busy day for me. I spent a great part of the 22nd and 23rd morning in making arrangements for the farewell party on the 23rd evening. Any event which is organized requires a lot of pre-event and post-event management. I personally attended to the arrangement of chairs in the pandal, decoration of tent and stage, arrangement of food stalls. I arranged the chairs for the faculty and the guests in the front, in a semi-circular shape. We had covered the path in the middle of the pandal with soft, red colored carpet.

At four in the afternoon, almost all the chairs were occupied, all the seats at the back were also filled. Students of my batch, my course mates and the colleagues in college, hung up to the banisters. I was the anchor of the event and my co-anchor was Purva. All that I can say about her is that she is a wonderful friend. That day she was dressed in a light green saree, beautifully worn in Saadhna style. I had put on a white-kurta with black jeans and a black scarf.

"We welcome all our sizzling seniors." I started with the welcome of the guests of the party. Purva my co-anchor, continued with the formal part. I never prepared the matter before going on for a show. The ideas which came on the spot were more attracting and creative. The stage to me was like a playground where I enjoyed the wittiness and spontaneity of words in my delivery. Purva handled the formal part and I was taking care of the informal anchoring.

In the third row on my right, when I was on stage, I saw Lisha sitting with a group of friends. She was beautifully dressed up in black. She looked damn hot and cute at the same time. She looked like a Barbie doll. We were able to make a few eye-contacts but now that I was the in-charge of the event, I had not much time to gaze on my beloved's face, although I was trying to dart glances in her direction. I even waved a 'Hi' once, when our eyes met and she smiled though without any feelings. I could sense that.

The party started with a big bang of heart breaking dance performances by seniors. A superb break dance was performed by two students. A group of ECE branch seniors made up the orchestra. Though they couldn't give the performance, the audience was expecting, they did give a start to the rap and the rock ambience for the people in the house. After every four cultural performances, we were engaging them with some party games like musical chairs, passing the parcel, finding the correct pair of footwear, etc-etc. It showed eight in the clock, when I noticed Lisha was not there in the pandal. I looked her for fifteen minutes but she was nowhere.

Finally, I called her up. "Where are you? I want to meet my favorite senior right now." I said in a pleading voice.

"Oh...I am sure you are having a great time hoisting the party."

"Lisha, I want to meet you." I repeated.

"*Chalo tumhe yaad to aayi*, but I am in hostel now. I am not feeling like coming back. Sorry..."

"Its okay Sweetheart. But *aaj to aapse milke hee rahunga*, I am coming to your room." I said in full confidence, as if the college was mine.

"Ah....I like that. Come then, I am waiting." she said and hung up.

Challenge to a son of Rajputana!! Now I had to enter the girl's hostel at any cost. But how?

A million thoughts went through my head, number one being, getting in with the mess workers. But the mess was on the ground floor and I had to reach the fourth floor. So the idea of getting in like a mess worker was drained. **Jonty Bhai**....!!! Yes, the idea took root in my mind.

I contacted the electrician, Jonty Bhai, to help me enter the girl's hostel. *"Arrey nahi, paagal ho kya?"* he said. Obviously, it was not an easy task. But it was the time when nothing was impossible for me, there was nothing in the world that I was not ready to try. I believed in the theory of three Ds. Well, let us not get into the theory of 3 Ds.

I passed a thousand rupee note to him and requested, I explained the urgency to him. He understood the problem and nodded to help me out in the matter. He was bought. I can be a good negotiator.....right?

Well, he provided me with a jute-handbag which contained a bunch of electric wires of the tri-color, green, red and black, a plier, a 40 watt bulb, a current tester, electric tape, fan regulator and some switch boards. He gave me his blue cap. I also borrowed a blue colored kurta from him, which had some green stains on it. He put some burnt oil and grease on my face, so that no one recognized me easily. And after the full make over, I could not recognize myself that it was me.

I knew I was attempting something for which if caught, I would be thrown out of the institute. But love had sharpened my wits. I entered the girl's hostel gate with Jonty bhai. My heart was pumping a hundred times faster than normal. We stepped into the main hostel building. Without looking here, we moved to the fourth floor straight away.

The fourth floor of the girl's hostel was for final year girls.

The wind was blowing in my direction. Luck was in. That evening the fourth floor was all empty as all the final year beauties had gone to the pandal for enjoying their farewell party.

"Avi Bhai I am going to the terrace to repair the boiler's connection. You get free by 8:30 positively. I will give you a missed call, yahi pe milna" Jonty Bhai instructed, wished me luck and moved to terrace. I moved towards the Lisha's apartment briskly. I entered the apartment. I was standing just in front of her door. I was very nervous and afraid of what I was doing and what I was about to do.

I was afraid of her reaction on seeing me in the girl's hostel, in her room. *Agar wo bahot tez chilla di to?*, I thought. I thought of returning back. But returning back at this stage could have never been my cup of tea. I mustered up all my courage and very boldly knocked on her door.

"Who's there?" she asked.

I didn't know what to say.

"*Kaun hai?*" she asked again, a bit irritatingly.

"Madam, *bijli check karni hai.*" I said in a very distorted tone.

"*ek minute rukna haan*" she said.

That one minute seemed like one year. My eyes were scanning any movements and my ears were sharply concentrating on the minutest of the noises. Thanks to the Almighty there was no disturbance.

After about eighty seconds she opened the door. Before she could understand anything, open her mouth, I shut her lips tightly with my hand. I entered in and latched the door.

"Please don't make any noise Lisha" I said and took my hand away.

"Avi, how come you are here? Are you crazy? What have you put on your face?" she was absolutely taken aback.

"Don't ask anything dear, I just managed to do it, somehow. I wanted to talk to you and you were not picking my call." I said with my eyes wet.

My heroic courage might have melted her heart to an extent.

"Are you out of your head? Koi aa gaya to you will be in great trouble. How did you come up?" she asked. She was frightened.

"Anything for you ma'am," in just four words I answered all the questions which were popping up in her mind.

"Avi, I'm afraid. Please go….."

"Please don't panic, I'll be off with Jonty Bhai within few minutes," I assured her.

She stood silent, totally tense.

Her room was exactly opposite to mine. It was a neat and tidy one. In my room, all my belongings were scattered make the room look small. Everything remained disordered. Clothes were strewn here and there. The hooks behind the door were always over-loaded with clothes. There was a book shelf but the majority of them the books were scattered on the bed, a couple of them on the study table and some on the cupboard and on the side table as well. Nothing was in its place. The study table was always flooded with files and papers. Posters, paper-cuttings and medals covered the four walls completely. Neha, one thing I would like to mention, my choice of selecting posters was quite different. I didn't like the Ferraris, or the Haptors or Britney. But I had put on posters of wacky quotations, motivational thoughts and of some eminent personalities.

I had kept a laundry bag in one corner of the room which remained flooded like a traffic jam on Howrah Bridge. If put on a weighing scale, it would have atleast shown twenty kilograms. Then there were my gadgets, a personal desktop computer with almost all the gadgets loaded. There were two keyboards, I remember, one was of the normal style and the other was the folding one. There were two mouses even, one was Microsoft's wireless optical mouse and the other one was the touch pad one. All the eight USB ports of my board remain occupied. Two of them were used by the wireless mouse connector and the folding keyboard. The third one was used by the TATA Indicom internet card. The fourth was for the web camera. The fifth port was for the printer, which most of the time remained out of cartridge. The sixth port was for an external hard-drive, 500 gigabytes. And the seventh & eight were left open for any extra peripherals to be used. Generally pen-drives took hold on them.

I was very fond of gadgets. You could find all the latest ones launched, with me. I just couldn't breath properly without them. I had even installed a 5.1 channel speaker system. The best of all was the wireless headphones, which had the acoustic cancellation technology. So, that completed the room of an Electronics & Communication engineering student.

Oops, I got diverted. So Neha, Lisha's room was a well set one. All her belongings had proper places. The stationery was confined to the study table only. No clothes could be spotted lying in the room. The bedsheet was neatly done. The pillow and quilt were kept in symmetry. She had even taken care of the color combinations even. Everything was so arranged!

"*Avi koi aa jayega*. Please go. *Ham pandal mei milte hain*" she requested in a deep voice. She even pushed me slightly.

"Lisha, I want to talk to you. Yahi pe." I said.

She remained silent.

"I am sorry for getting angry with you unnecessarily. I am really sorry for the way the last two months have passed" I said.

She closed her eyes and said "And I am really sorry for reacting the negative way….. but I really didn't liked the way you reacted, the way you avoided me." and she started crying.

I too felt very emotional and some drops of tears appeared in my eyes.

"Lisha, I love you and I'll love you always" I said and folded her in my arms. We cried together on each others shoulders for the next two minutes. I managed to get a control on my emotions and then helped her to do so too.

I made her sit on the chair, wiped her tears off. Then I bent down to my knees. I took her hand in mine and presented her the ring with a soft kiss on her fist. "Dear, I want to spend my whole life with you. Will you marry me?"

She brightened up. The saddy-saddy tears got converted to the happy-happy ones, though they started coming out in larger numbers.

"Yes, I will" she said accepting the ring, going pink as always. She stood up and I followed. Then she kissed me full on the mouth. I was surprised, I could tell from the way her eyes widened just before our lips made contact. She looked up at me, though it wasn't easy for her. Then her gaze slid and she released a little, only to realize that she was then looking at my lips.

I stopped being surprised pretty quick and it ended up a nice long kiss.

Her touch made me feel in the seventh heaven. I was only conscious of her soft movements then. All my thought diverted on her golden touch. She threw her arms around my neck and we again kissed.

All the emotions within us started pouring out.

"Your hair's so soft" I said.

She gave a deadly stare. It drove my heart far away from the world. Instantly the world became a better place.

"Lisha, I missed your touch since the last two months. I was missing you badly when I was on stage today. You were looking so pretty in a black saree, I wanted to kiss you and tell you." I touched the center of her lower lip gently with one calloused thumb.

"Right here." But then she said "But I am not going to, okay!"

Her *okay* sounded as a question to me, whose answer was obviously 'not'.

I picked her up in an effort to silence her and I started licking her face thoroughly. She kissed my forehead and smiled. Her smile gave me the green signal of proceeding ahead. I lifted her off her feet. An extremely undignified little struggle followed where she tried to move to the study table and I tried to carry her, and it basically ended with her sort of stumbling up, breathless, hair everywhere.

I had my arms around her waist and I was looking down at her, smiling very fondly. We looked connected.

My cell phone buzzed, obviously not with a ring as I had put it on the vibration mode. I didn't bother to check it. I was completely lost in her love.

"You were here to talk to me, right?" she said.

"Who said I wanted to talk to you?" I said and calmly started kissing her exposed shoulder. She opened her mouth in protest but I placed a finger on her lips and looked down at her, the smile quite gone from her face. I could feel her hands trembling, just a little. And then, very deliberately I rose up a little to kiss her.

It was like all of me rose up and surged to my lips, as if my life source was where her mouth was, as if her soul was on her lips and I was kissing it. My large warm hand had slid under her shirt and settled tantalizingly right over her madly thumping heart but made no attempt at exploring the rest of her.

"In spite of all your big talks, you are such a little girl" I said.

"If you care to move your hand on either side, just a little, you would be provided with substantial proof that I am quite a big girl after all" she said feeling mortified.

I laughed softly and shook my head, sliding my hand way up, so that my fingers appeared through the neckline of her top.

And then suddenly we heard somebody calling her name. *Lisha......Lishaaaaa* the voice was getting louder and louder. "Avi run! Go and hide yourself in the loo....Oh God! I told you na". She got frightened and very tense.

I ran away to the bathroom and latched the door from inside. Instantly the world became the worst place.

"Yes Ma'am" she answered the call.

"Where were you? I was searching for you." said the warden.

"I was just resting, I was very tired." she made a comfortable excuse.

"Whatever. Now go to apartment number 416 for an urgent meeting" the warden ordered.

"What happened ma'am? Some ragging case?" Lisha enquired.

"No, it is much serious. Half an hour ago two electricians entered and only one amongst them has gone out."

"What? What about the other one?" Lisha asked. I was listening to their conversation from inside the loo.

"And we have even come to know that the other one is not an electrician, he is some out-sider."

I cursed Jonty Bhai as he moved out, leaving me behind. How could he do that? Why didn't he inform me? I was questioning to myself. I decided to call him up and ask for my rescue. My cell phone showed thirteen missed calls. All of them were Jonty bhai's. Crap....!! He had called me up. He must have tried for more than fifteen minutes, at least. God damn... what was I supposed to do!!!

"The management and the guards will be reaching in five minutes. So assemble in 416" the warden informed her and went off. Tears sprang Lisha's eyes.

Luck was out. The wind had start blowing in the other way now. She knocked on my door.

"Avi come out." I opened the door and came out. I could see terror in her eyes.

"How will you go now?" she cried.

"Don't panic, don't panic. Let me think." I said, panting.

"Avi, the guards must have reached."

"Go get me a dupatta…..fast" I ordered. I don't know what was there in my mind.

She ran into her room and brought it. I took it from her hurriedly and then rushed to the balcony at the opposite face of the hostel.

"What the hell are you trying to do? Don't be crazy Avi" she shouted.

I put my legs over the balcony's railing, kissed her forehead and said "Lisha, just after two minutes you throw a bucket half filled with water from the front balcony. Do it from some other apartment. Meet you tomorrow Sweetie" and I slipped down making full use of the gaps in the bricked wall, the parallel iron bars in the balconies and the dupatta to get support.

Lisha must have thrown the bucket well on time because no one appeared at the back side of the hostel to check for the *out-sider*, and I could comfortably move down. Though it was a MI-2 job but I was happy that I was not caught. My idea of throwing the bucket worked. I had asked for that to create confusion amongst the guards and the management. The bucket must have diverted their mind. Yes, it all worked as per the plan.

When I touched ground, I felt like I had completed some 007 mission. I looked up to the fourth floor to take a last glance of hers, but she was not there. I quickly jumped off the hostel boundary from the back and ran away.

I took hardly five minutes to get dressed up again, for the show. I returned to the pandal and then to the stage to join the ongoing party.

Purva, my co-anchor had handled the stage quite well. The audience was still into the show. The heat was on!

"Where had you gone?" she asked.

I just smiled. I had nothing to answer actually. *Chori agar pakdi na jaye to maza aa jaata hai,* I was recalling the last hour. I was not able to believe to what I had done. I went on to the stage and continued........

I could see many of the senior faculty members missing. Probably they had all gone to check out the 'out-sider electrician' matter.

One plus One = One

3 0th April 2005, Annual General Meet of Institution of Engineers (India) DIT Chapter was being held in the seminar hall of our college. Eminent personalities like Er. Prakash Singh (Chief Engineer THDC), Er. K.P Uniyal (MD Jal Nigam Uttarakhand), Er. K.C Goel, Prof. K.P Brar, Prof. Shankar Kumar, Dr. Ravi Kumar and Prof. Gajendra Sharma were the guest of honors.

Well known persons like DC, Aditya, Ria, Nehal, Manpreet, Ntini, Piyush were helping with the arrangements. I am calling them great because they were the true treasures and ideal examples of friendship in my life. Another eminent personality made herself comfortable in the audience. As from there she could maintain a direct eye-contact with me. Lisha left no opportunity when she could make me feel conscious. She enjoyed it a lot. Passing me the flying kisses, doing uncensored actions just to divert my attention while I was on stage, was her favorite pastime.

I always got diverted whenever Lisha came in my mind.

Well in about thirty minutes all the arrangements were made and Prof. Gajendra Sharma started with the welcoming of the audience. He then introduced the functioning and working of IE(I), DIT Chapter.

I was sure that no body listened to it.

The progress report of the IE(I), DIT Chapter was then read by the former Student President of the club. After finishing the report he invited the Chief Guest on the dais to declare the new Student President for Institution of Engineers (India) for the next academic session.

"Good fortune searches out the people who have the indomitable spirit as well as an unremitting zeal" Er. Uniyal started.

"Now I announce name of such a person who really has an indomitable spirit and undying enthusiasm." said he.

"So, friends. Please join your hands to welcome Mr. Avinash Jain of Electronics Final Year, here on the stage to hold the post of Student President of IE(I) DIT Chapter" he said in a loud pitch.

The hall roared with clapping. My friends started patting me for the very prestigious achievement. Everybody started congratulating me. "Thanks", "Thank you very much" was what I was saying to everyone.

I was supposed to be very happy. I was supposed to have sparkle in my eyes but instead, there was just a blank look.

All along, there had been so many tragedies in my life. The days when I got expelled from the hostel were being recalled. The days when my parents had been called to the college because of the offence I had committed appeared as a clear picture right in front of me. I was both happy and sad at the same time. I was thinking of my parents at that point of time. I just wished they were here in Dehradun to see me getting honors from my college management. I wanted everyone to realize what I had achieved. I wanted all my friends, relatives, and all the other people whom I have met even once to join the celebration. I was happy to be honored for such a post, as I had seen so many ups and downs during college life.

Leaving all thoughts behind, I walked towards the stage.

My bio-data was being read.

"Avinash Jain who is now the new Student President of IE(I) DIT Chapter had never been ready with little gracious acts. Right from his childhood in Apeejay School,Noida, he has been a great innovator. Avinash has desires for the weapon of learning for practical ends. His service as a laborer is considerable. His energy level is prodigious. His team work and leadership has set wonderful examples for all the people around him. Avinash is also the Chairperson and President of the All Round Development Club" narrated Prof. Sharma. He went on giving an impressive history of my upbringing, ranging over twenty years.

I was on the stage to receive the honor. Photographers were flashing their cameras continuously, as if they were ordered to shoot each and every expression of mine. All my friends were cheering at the top of their voices. The faculty members present and other guests were giving huge applauses.

But I could see an unusual silence in the cheering crowd. Lisha still remained on her seat, she didn't have any expression of joy. It seemed like she had got some unbearable shock. No, obviously not because I was selected as the President but there was sure to have been some other reason. While receiving the honor I looked at her, made an eye-contact and smiled.

She didn't respond.

Instantly after receiving the award, I was called to the podium to answer some of the questions from the student audience.

Answering to questions on stage, making announcements in lecture halls, giving speeches, motivating students to work in a team have became very common for me. Not even taking a clocks tick time, I confidently marched to the podium.

"Avinash, your colleagues, your juniors and the faculty staff finds you the most successful student of the institute. What do you feel about it? ", was the first question thrown at me after receiving the post of the Student President of IE(I) DIT Chapter.

"Success to me is about attaining a certain sensibility that one finds within oneself. This sensibility is something I cannot measure or define. It is about a particular moment, an instance, an expression, an experience that is realized." I answered.

Everyone clapped. My friends who were sitting in the audience applauded loudly and largely. I was trying to catch Lisha's eye while speaking but she didn't look at me.

"To me every individual is inherently special and successful in some way or the other. I have been fortunate to receive several accolades and I am thankful for all of them. But these can only provide momentary sensations of happiness or success. All the attention, awards and recognition actually brings along a strong sense of responsibility of meeting millions of expectations." I added.

"Sir, do you think that competitions are the right process for enhancing talent?" asked someone from the Editorial Board of the college.

"When it comes to competition, I feel it is a healthy way of ensuring the development and growth of societies. We should always be inspired and enthusiastic about evolving and climbing further and further up the ladder of development. We must not stuck up with the dark days of our life rather learn lessons" replied me.

I guess that would have worked as a motivational statement to be put up in the Ed-Board's magazine. The questioning session got over and I was greatly praised on the way I answered. People were amazed to listen to the content I delivered in my answers. To be very true I knew what all questions were to be asked, so I had already prepared the answers a day before.

Well, when the felicitation ceremony got over, gradually the audience started moving out. I got busy with my fellow students and faculty members who were congratulating me for the very achievement. But Lisha didn't come. I was looking for her continuously but she managed to escape with the audience. I was not able to judge her reaction. Was she planning a surprise for me? Or was she really upset with something?

Thousands of questions ran through my mind of what might have been the reason of Lisha leaving the hall in such a manner. I was on the stage so couldn't catch a hold on her and make out the actual reason behind.

As the function got over I got surrounded by all my friends. "Congratulations dude!", "Where's the party tonight?" roared many of them all together.

"Where ever and when ever you want." I replied. But my eyes were searching for her.

What could have happened? Was she not feeling well?

After the crowd cleared, I rushed to the corridor to see if Lisha was waiting. But I couldn't find her there. I searched all the corridors, the one going to the Physics department, the one of Chemistry department and even the ones going to Humanities and Computer Science departments, but I couldn't spot her.

I rushed to the terrace. Because, terrace was the place where we used to sit many times. It was the place where we had all the serious discussions, where we used to disclose the surprises for each other, where we sat for hours just to see into each others eyes. It was the place where we used to den when we wanted no one around. We used to decide our present and even the future there.

And as per my expectations, I found her there. But this time she was not alone, she was sitting with some girl. Both had their backs to the entrance to the stairs of the terrace.

"Lisha!" I called in low voice, standing on the last stair-step itself.

Lisha turned around. Tears were rolling down her eyes.

"What happened?" I rushed towards her.

She broke off badly in tears. Without thinking of anything else I grabbed her in my arms.

"*Cheeku!* Oh come-on stop crying."

"*Beta* I am here now. Your Avi is here for you. Tell me what the matter is. Is something wrong? Why did you leave the Hall without even meeting me? You didn't even see me taking the award on the stage. What happened?" I asked in a low voice. "And by the way who's she?"

Lisha managed to stop her tears. She remained silent and kept looking at me. "She is my friend." she answered.

"Is everything okay at home?" enquired me.

"Avi I can't believe this!" She kept on crying.

"What? What is that you can't believe?" asked me.

She was silent and kept looking directly into my eyes.

"I became President is what you can't believe!"

"Avi, I can't believe that you are Avinash Jain who had once studied in Apeejay Noida." she said.

"Stop it Cheeku! What is so strange about Apeejay that you can't believe?" I was puzzled.

"I can't believe that you are Avi, Lenika's Avi." she said.

"What?" I was shocked and surprised. "Lenika! Lisha what is the matter? Please do tell me." I urged.

She closed her eyes.

I remained silent. I was waiting for her to say something.

"Don't you remember Lenika Avinash?"

"Yes when you mentioned Apeejay, I recalled. She was my best friend. I used to tease her, make fun of her and she never took an edge below. She always fought back. I liked her. But how do you get to know about her?"

Lisha held my hand and pulled me close to her friend sitting with her back at our side. Her friend was wearing blue jeans with a white top. She was sitting still as if she didn't realize our presence. "She is my friend Avi. She is doing architecture from our college" Lisha introduced me to her friend.

I was confused as to what was happening. Why did Lisha come to terrace with her friend whom I have never seen before? Why did she cry badly? Why did she introduce me to her friend? How was I connected with all this?

"Hello....umm What's your name?" I said.

"Lenika" she said.

"What?" I was in deep shock. I was taken aback. "Is this some prank Lisha?"

"No Avi. She is Lenika your childhood friend" Lisha said.

My heart froze. Veins and arteries seemed to have never existed. I was not ready to believe my eyes and ears. I kept on looking at Lenika, my eyes didn't blink.

Lenika ran away from there. I was left alone. Ya, I didn't even felt the presence of Lisha. It was for the first time I remember that I didn't feel her presence.

"Avi. Where are you lost? What's on your mind?" Lisha asked.

"Lisha I am not able to believe all this. I want to talk to her. Why did she run away?" I was totally confused. "I hope you are not kidding." I said.

"Avi, your Lenika is in our college," she stressed.

I don't understand why Lisha was saying *your Lenika* again and again. Was she jealous of her? Jealous of my childhood friend? Or jealous of my childhood love.......my first love?

I was actually dying to meet Lenika. Was the presence of Lenika in my own college true? Well, I gathered all my senses and started reacting the mature way.

"Okay forget all this. Tell me why you didn't introduce Lenika to me in the seminar hall itself? Why did you not come up? And why did you cry?" I asked all the unanswered questions that were running in my mind, in one go.

"Because.......Avi, tell me one thing honestly". Lisha was still not in a good mood.

"What? Lisha what has happened to you?" I asked.

"Lenika loves you Avi, she told me." Lisha said.

"What? Lisha please stop it now." I said irritably.

"No, please let me complete. If she proposes to you, what will your answer be Avi?" she asked something which I had never expected her to. I never knew that one day our relationship would take such a turn. Why did she put me in such situation? I was not able to react. I had nothing to say. On one side I had found my childhood friend whom I loved a lot, whom I actually missed for years and on the other hand was my present. Neha, for the whole god damn life I had been able to make all kind of excuses but this time I had nothing to say.

On one hand was Lisha, my love, for whom I had waited for years and on the other hand was Lenika, my childhood love, which was very innocent and pure.

"What are you thinking of, Avi?" she asked.

"I need some time. Please leave me alone." I requested. Actually I was trying to avoid the confrontation.

"What do you need time for? Are you confused? Avi please be honest with yourself. Tell me who's on your mind and in your heart? Tell me now."

"Lisha I love you. How can you even think of relating yourself with someone? But definitely yes, meeting Lenika again after fifteen years is the role of destiny. There must be some relation or link. There would certainly be some divine reason for such a coincidence" I said.

"Please give me some time. I respect Lenika's feeling for me and I love you very much. I don't want to hurt any of you." I spoke out my heart.

Lisha's eyes became moist. She stood straight and expressionless. It seemed as if she was about to faint. "Lisha, I am sorry….. I am hurting you." I said breaking the silence.

"No Avi its ok. I am happy that you are being honest." she said. I closed my eyes. I was not able to face her.

For the next few minutes no one said anything. Lisha was trying to look straight into my eyes, while I was trying to hide from her. She was waiting for my answer. And I was looking down, motionless.

All of a sudden she exclaimed with great joy, "Yes Avi, meeting you after fifteen years is the role of destiny. I love you Avi" she shouted like she had won some jackpot and hugged me.

I was completely surprised at her reaction. A minute ago she had tears in her eyes and now she jumped in joy.

"You *White Panty*. I can't believe that you are the Avinash who put tadpoles inside my top." she screamed.

"What?" this time a big one. I was surprised.

Lisha knew the name with which Lenika used to call me.

She kissed on my cheek and said "Ya, this is your Lenika, my sweetie pie!" pointing to herself.

Everything seemed to freeze for the next few minutes.

"Lenika?" I questioned towards pointing her. "Who was she?"

"Shut up you dumbo…. *Mere pyare dhakkan.* Don't you realize that.."

"That?" I asked.

"That this Lisha was your childhood friend Lenika. She was Sneha, just a friend of mine. I asked her to pretend to be that." she said.

I was still not able to get the things clearly.

"Avi, I just wanted to test you. I wanted to know whether you loved me fifteen years back or not. I wanted to test your honesty. You are so pure at heart. I love you." she screamed.

"Lisha….you want to say that you are Lenika! I mean….."

"Yes Avi, I am your Lenika only. There was a misprint, *Lisha* instead of *Lenika* in my tenth class scorecard, after which I had to use Lisha as my name in all the records" she smiled.

I pinched myself just to make sure that I was not dreaming. It pained, thereby confirming the scene I was in. I was not able to believe to it. *Lisha was Lenika!!!* God….what was happening!!!

"Yeah I loved you Lisha….no Lenika…..uff! Lenika…..Lisha?" I was puzzled.

I found myself dumbstruck. I couldn't utter a word. The excitement surged in me. I was bathed in white light.

"Don't say anything Avi. God has made us meet this way." she said placing her index finger on my lips.

I took both her hands in mine and then brought her closer and she submitted herself to my arms. I hugged her. I hugged her warmly, as tightly as I could. It was difficult for me to believe my eyes. I was not able to analyze to what all happening with me was a dream or reality. I tightened my grip in folding her. I could feel her breathing against my chest. I felt something wet on my neck. I released her a little and saw her tears. Some tears were still trickling down her cheek.

Again I folded her in my arms. I moved my lips close to hers. They touched and then mingled. We kept on kissing, the wind, the sky, the day, had all ceased to exist.

"So, where's she now? Why didn't you tell your parents about Lisha?" Neha asked.

I am
still ALIVE

It was june 2005 when Lisha's course got finished. She passed out from college and I entered my final year of engineering. She got a job in Delhi, her hometown.

I used to make frequent visits from Dehradun to Delhi to meet her. She didn't like me missing the college and doing 500 kms up-down just to meet her. In spite of her repeated requests, I used to meet her, atleast once in every fortnight. We used to spend time together in malls, we used to watch movies, we used to go to gardens. One day she even introduced me to her parents. We went out for a family picnic. Earlier I was finding it very uncomfortable to be with her family but her parents were very nice to me and we had a great time together. Her father shared roaring laughters on my jokes. Her mother was treating me as if she had already accepted me as her daughter's husband. Everything went off so well.

Three months passed.

It was the last week of October. I had planned a surprise visit to Delhi to meet her. It was for the first time that I had not given Lisha prior information of my visit. I was a bit tense, what if Lisha is not in town? What if she is not able to take leave from her work? Avi, inform her or else your surprise visit might become a surprise for yourself! I was talking to myself.

Killing all my dilemmas, I boarded the bus from Doon to Delhi at 10:45 in night.

At around 2'O clock, my cellphone buzzed.

"Avi, there is a good news" she exclaimed.

"What?" I asked.

"I'll tell you, but you have to meet me" she said.

"Oh ho Lisha aisee kya baat hai?"

"Tum bas miloge mujhe, no excuses okay!" she ordered.

"But betu I am in Doon......." I said.

"Kal 2 baje."

"Lisha...are you nuts? Howz that possible? I mean......I can't." I said, though I was about to reach Delhi in four hours.

"Hundreds of times I stop you for not coming to my place, but you come. And now when I need to tell you something then you are making excuses." she said in a low voice, and then started crying.

"Achha baba I am coming. Stop crying now." I said. She spoiled the surprise which I was supposed to give.

"Shoppers Stop, Ansal Plaza at 2 sharp." she said.

"Why at two? Why not in the morning?" I asked.

"Morning?? How come? You will atleast take seven hours to reach my dear." she said in a convincing tone.

"I was not supposed to tell you but sweetheart I was in my way to Delhi, I had planned a surprise for you" I said.

"What?? Avi, you are.......you are my real Hero.

180

Mmmmmmuuuuaaaahhhh" and she gave a smacking kiss.

"I won't spare you this time. You are spoiling your career." she said, with full-on *nakhre*.

"Arrey, but you were supposed to give me good news." I reminded.

"That I will but after breaking your head."

"I love you Lisha." I said.

"Love you too mere buddhu......meet me at 11 at Ansals....okay?"

"Okay Dear.....Miss you." I said.

"Miss you too..........bye."

I reached Ansal Plaza one hour earlier and waited patiently for her. As the time was passing by my heart had started beating faster. I was anxiously waiting for her. It struck 11:30, but she was nowhere to be seen. After looking for her for ten more minutes, I dialled her number.

"Hello....Lisha. Where are you?"

"Bas sweetheart reaching in fifteen minutes, I have reached Sarojini Nagar"

"Okay, come inside Shoppers Stop" I said.

"mmmmmuuuuaaahhhhh.........bye" she kissed me and hung off.

I was wandering around in the store to find out something good for her, to celebrate the good news she was about to tell. Thirty minutes passed but she didn't come.

You know Neha, Lisha was always like that, she never used to be on time. But I liked that too. So, that day, I was patiently waiting for her.

Another thirty minutes passed and there was no indication from her side.

After about twenty minutes more, I gave up. My patience was gone. I called her up.

She didn't take the call. And then all of a sudden it went out-of-range.

I tried again and again, but the connection could not be made. I got tensed.

I called up her home.

"Hello....Aunty? Is Lisha at home?" I asked in a hurry, as soon as she picked up the reciever.

And I heard a terrifying cry. Aunty cried like something very wrong had happened. I could sense the terror in her voice.

"Aunty...hello...aunty...." The line got disconnected. I quickly ran out of the store to board a bus for her home.

I called up again, "Aunty, what happened? Why are you crying? Is everything fine?" I asked.

She broke down.

"Aunty please stop crying, please tell me what the matter is?"

"Beta Sarojini Nagar mei blast........" she said and stopped saying anything all of a sudden.

It was frightenng. "Aunty...what blast? Aunty please tell me" I urged. But I didn't get any reply.

I could make out that something was wrong.

I hired a taxi and reached her home. When I entered her home, I saw Lisha's mother lying on floor. She was in semiconscious state.

I helped her to sit. "Aunty kya hua? Whats the matter? Where is Lisha?"

"Sarojini Nagar.....bomb.......she is no more." she said and fainted.

I fell on my knees.

After picking myself up, I called up her relatives and we rushed to the hospital.

Her body was not found.

Neha, till today, I don't know what that good news was. Lisha left me forever.

And Avinash closed his eyes, in deep pain. Tears formed a continuous stream down his face. Neha was shocked to hear the tragic end of the lovely couple. She too was drowned in tears. And then she held Avinash's hand, tightly......and then hugged him.

"Avinash, if not as your love, I'd like to be your life partner as a friend." said Neha, in a heavy whisper.

www.ingramcontent.com/pod-product-compliance
Lightning Source LLC
Chambersburg PA
CBHW051657260626
47170CB00004B/1556